At that moment the six-foot, four-inch frame of a man wearing what looked to be a white toga came flying past the window outside.

"Wa-wa-wa," the man called as he zoomed upward toward the roof.

Remo looked to the snow-covered garden below, already sure of who would be down there.

A crowd of onlookers near the swimming pool, similarly attired and shivering in the cold, gasped and shrieked piteously as a second man blasted off into space. In the center of the throng stood Chiun, his arms folded triumphantly across his chest, his face serene.

"Oh, bulldookey," Remo sighed. The first man turned an arc overhead and began his dive, nose first, like a white-sheathed warhead. His features were set rigidly in a mask of unadulterated terror as he sped downward alongside the house.

"Hang on!" Remo called, throwing open the window and hoisting himself up to his knees.

"To what?" the man moaned.

"To me." He stretched out his arms, slowly pivoting so that he was facing up, supported by the backs of his knees against the window frame. He was directly in line with the falling body.

A woman below screamed and fainted. "This is terrible," another said.

"Quite terrible," Chiun said sympathetically. "Remo is always interfering."

"How could you do such a thing?" a muscular beach-blanket type yelled to Chiun.

"Oh, it was nothing," he said, beaming modestly. "Just a small upward thrust. It is an elementary maneuver. . . ."

THE DESTROYER SERIES:

The Destroyer

Warren Murphy

#50

GOLDEN EDITION

KILLING TIME

PINNACLE BOOKS **NEW YORK**

For Regina Caroselli
Often thought of
and the house of Sinanju
P. O. Box 1454,
Secaucus, N.J. 07092

THE DESTROYER #50: KILLING TIME

An original Pinnacle Books edition, published for the first time anywhere.

First printing, October, 1982

ISBN: 0-523-41560-5

Cover illustration by Hector Garrido

Printed in the United States of America

PINNACLE BOOKS, INC.
1430 Broadway
New York, New York 10018

KILLING TIME

Chapter One

The vintage 1940 Rolls-Royce Silver Shadow glided noiselessly through New York's Central Park, its smoked windows sealing off the lilting strains of Pachelbel's *Canon* from the humdrum sounds of the city.

Inside, behind the liveried chauffeur, sitting in a sea of velvet the color of his dark wavy hair, Dr. Felix Foxx sipped at a daiquiri from a glass of cut Baccarat crystal. He pressed a button on the partition between the front and rear seats.

"Any joggers?" he asked the chauffeur.

"No, sir."

"Keep looking," Foxx said in richly modulated tones, and switched the microphone off.

Ah, this was the life, he thought as he sniffed a rose in its Lalique bud vase. He finished his drink and set the glass back into the small lacquer bar built into the Rolls. He slid his hand over his $55 tie from Tripler and the flawlessly tailored lapels of his $1200 Lanvin suit. He looked down at his Botticelli shoes, gleaming a dark mahogany against the white plush of the carpeting.

A perfect life.

1

The rear speakers buzzed to attention. "Joggers, sir."

Foxx's eyes narrowed into hard little slits. "Where?"

"Ahead and to the left, Dr. Foxx."

He peered through the darkened glass. Ahead, running alongside the road, were a man and woman dressed in running clothes, their Adidas sneakers kicking up the dust behind them. Their faces were flushed and glistening with sweat.

"Get into position," he said.

The car sped up alongside the joggers, then spurted slightly ahead. "Ready?' Foxx asked, a small spark of lust coming to his eyes.

"Ready, sir."

Through the smoked windows of the Rolls, Foxx took a good look at the joggers. They were sparkling with good health, two fine specimens flirting with one another. "Now," he growled.

The car zoomed forward, kicking up a cloud of dirt and pebbles onto the astonished joggers. Through the rear window, Foxx could see them coughing and sputtering, their shiny perspiring faces coated with soot.

"On target," he yelled, laughing uproariously.

"Yes, sir," the chauffeur said.

"Shut up." He slammed off the communications system and chuckled while he took out a silver vial from his vest pocket and snorted a noseful of cocaine from a tiny silver spoon.

He hated joggers. He hated health. If it weren't for the millions brought in from *Running & Relativity* and *Live Free On Celery*—Foxx's two books concurrently on the *New York Times* bestseller list—he'd see to it that runners, hikers, dancercisers, tennis players, ski bunnies, and all the assorted other health nuts of the world were put on priority lists for euthanasia.

The car swept out of the park and pulled up slowly beside the curb. "It's two blocks to the television studio, sir," the chauffeur said.

Foxx sighed and put away the cocaine vial with a growl. "All right, all right," he said with the resignation of the doomed. "Hand them over."

The sliding partition behind the driver slid open, and the chauffeur handed him a neatly stacked pile of clothing. There was an undershirt, a pair of pale blue custom-tailored sweatpants, and a jacket to match. Foxx unfastened his own clothing reluctantly and handed it up to the driver, then put on the running clothes with a grimace. He hated the feel of them.

"Sweat," he commanded morosely.

Obediently, the driver handed him an atomized bottle of Evian Tonique Refraisant, which Foxx dutifully sprayed over his face to simulate perspiration.

It was hell being a health guru. "Anyone around?" he asked.

"Coast is clear, sir." The chauffeur slid out of his seat and came around to open the door for Foxx.

"Pick me up in an hour," Foxx said. He retched once and trotted away.

By the time he reached the WACK studios, the retching had subsided and the expression of bitter resolution on his face had changed to one of radiant cheer. He waved to onlookers outside the studio entrance. He joked with the receptionist in the studio. He told funny stories to the other guests waiting to go on the "Frank Diamond Show" in the studio's green room. He jogged triumphantly on stage.

On camera, he was greeted with shouts and cheers. Frank Diamond introduced him as "Felix Foxx, the Phantom of Fitness."

Smiling warmly, he admonished the overweight housewives of the nation to find happiness through fitness and his books. Audience members gave testimony to the life-changing effects of Dr. Foxx's inspirational talks. Middle-aged women screamed in ecstasy as he demonstrated jumping jacks. Fat girls threw their candy bars into the aisles with the fervor of zealots.

At the stage door exit after the show, a group of adoring fans thrust copies of *Running & Relativity* and *Live Free on Celery* at him to sign. Among the flapping pages was a pair of oversized breasts thinly covered by a tight pink sweater. Foxx followed the breasts upward to a Shirley Temple face beneath a mop of curly blonde hair.

"Hi," the girl breathed, causing her sweater to stretch almost beyond endurance. "I think you're just fabulous, Dr. Foxx," she whispered. Her lips quivered.

"Oh?" Foxx said. She looked like the sort of girl who could accommodate him. Not many could. The last had been a screamer. Screamers were out.

"Have you read my books?"

"No. I'm waiting for the movie to come out." She pushed ahead of her a frowzy redhead with a road map face covered by thick layers of pancake. "This here's my roommate Doris. We live together. She thinks you're cute, too."

"Really," Foxx said, aghast. As he signed more autographs, he contemplated the blonde girl's mouth. It curved upward, like a new moon. There were bruises on her neck. "Where did you get those?" he asked, brushing his hand languidly along her throat as the autograph seekers moaned in longing.

"Oh. My boyfriend," she giggled. "He gets kind of rough sometimes. It turns me on."

That was it, Foxx decided. She would do. "You'd better get a doctor to look at that," he said.

"Oh, it's nothing," the girl gushed. "Just a bruise. I get them all the time." Doris poked her in the ribs. "Oh. Did I say something wrong? Doris says I'm always saying stupid things."

"My dear, you're enchanting," Foxx said. "Let me look at those bruises."

Her eyes rounded. "You mean you're a real doctor? Like on 'General Hospital'?"

"That's right." He eased her through the crowd toward the Rolls parked outside. "That's all, ladies," he said charmingly to the throng. "I've got a small emergency to take care of."

The women sighed in disappointment. One of them shouted that she loved him. He took the woman's hand and squeezed it. "Be the best you can be," he said earnestly. The women squealed with delight.

Inside the car, Foxx offered the blonde a glass of champagne. "I just love this fizzy stuff," she said. "Once I broke my arm. I took an Alka Seltzer. It felt wonderful."

"Your broken arm?"

She laughed wildly. "No, silly. The fizz. The arm didn't feel like anything at all."

Foxx stiffened. "Wasn't there any pain?"

"Nope. A guy I knew once—he worked in a carnival—he said there was a name for people like me. You know, people who don't feel pain. It's weird, I was always like that. . . ."

"A horse," Foxx said, staring fixedly at the girl. She

was everything he wanted. Everything. And more.

"Hey, that's right. A horse. That's what he said. Maybe you know him. Johnny Calypso, the Tattooed Man."

"Mmm. I doubt it," Foxx muttered. It was going to be a wonderful evening.

The Rolls pulled up in front of an awning in the expensive section of Fifth Avenue, and a doorman strode forward to help them out. "Oh, by the way, my name's Irma," the girl said. "Irma Schwartz."

"Lovely," Foxx said.

Irma was a dynamo. Foxx started with clothespins and graduated steadily through needles, ropes, whips, chains, and fire. "Does it hurt yet?" Foxx wheezed, exhausted.

"No, Doc," Irma said, swigging from the bottle of champagne she'd brought with her from the car. "I told you. I'm a horse."

"You're a sensation."

"So are you, Foxie. Running changed my life. Really. Last week. Before that, I was into roller skating, only I broke my nose. I couldn't smell too good out of it, so I got it fixed. Before that, I was into rolfing. And est. Only I quit that 'cause I didn't like people calling me an asshole. I mean, getting beat up by your boyfriend's one thing, but when a total stranger calls you an asshole, you know—"

"Didn't the broken nose hurt, either?" Foxx asked, yanking at her hair.

" 'Course not. I told you, I don't feel nothing. Then before that, the est I mean, I was into Valiums. But I started eating a lot. Doris, my roommate, told me how the guys at the Metropole was saying I was getting fat."

"Metropole," Foxx muttered as he dug his teeth into Irma's shoulder.

"That's where I work. I'm a go-go dancer. They couldn't believe it when I wrote down on the application how old I was. Bet you can't guess, either."

"I don't care." He was on his way to paradise again.

"Go ahead. Guess."

Foxx sat up with a sigh. "All right. Twenty? Twenty-five?"

"Forty-three."

Foxx inhaled deeply. "Forty-three?" There were no lines on her face, no trace that Irma Schwartz had been on the planet longer than two decades. "You really are a horse," he mused. "The rarest kind of horse."

"I read a thing about it once in Ripley's *Believe It or Not*. There's some kind of drug in me. Not that I put it there on purpose or nothing, it's just there. Doctors call it propane."

"Procaine," Foxx corrected abstractly. His mind was racing. Irma Schwartz was too good to be true. What she possessed was worth more than all the nookie in the world. It would be selfish to keep her to himself. She belonged to the world.

"Yeah, that's it. Procaine."

"You're very lucky," he said. "People pay thousands of dollars for what you've got. A lot of forty-three-year-old women would like to look like they're twenty. It's an age retardant. Procaine's been used by the military for years. In small amounts, it wards off pain. It's related to Novocaine and to cocaine, only the human body produces it. In larger quantities, the drug can slow down the aging process. Theoretically, it can actually stop aging completely, allowing people to stay young for their entire lives. Of course, that's only theory. It's much too rare to use in quantities like that."

"Well, how do you like that?" Irma said. "I got something floating around inside me that's worth money."

"Lots of money," Foxx said. "Any clinic in Europe would pay a fortune for the procaine in your system."

"Yeah?" Irma brightened. "Maybe I can sell some. I mean, I got lots, right?"

Foxx smiled. "I'm afraid that would be impossible. You'd have to be dead to donate it."

Irma giggled. "Oh. Well, I guess it's back to dancing at the Metropole."

Foxx dug his thumbnail into her ear in a gesture of endearment. Irma giggled. "Be right back," he said. He returned a moment later.

His hands were sheathed in rubber gloves. In his left hand was a brown, medicinal-looking bottle. In his right, a thick wad of cotton.

"What's that?" Irma asked.

"Something to make you crazy."

"Like drugs?"

"Like." He poured some of the contents of the bottle onto the cotton wool. The fumes stung his eyes and made his breathing catch.

"You're really good to me, you know that?" Irma tittered. "I mean, champagne, now this. . . ."

"Breathe deeply," Foxx said.

She did. "I'm not getting off."

"You will."

"This the new thing at the discos?"

"The latest. They say it's like dying and going to heaven."

"What's it called?" Irma asked, her eyes rolling.

"Prussic acid."

"Groovy," Irma Schwartz said before she died.

Chapter Two

His name was Remo and he was climbing an electrified fence. He'd had trouble before with electricity, but after the old man had shown him how to conquer it, the matter of scaling a twelve-foot high screen of electrified mesh was no problem. The trick was to use the electricity.

Most people fought against the current, just as they fought against gravity when trying to climb. The old man had shown Remo long ago that gravity was a force too strong for any man to fight, and that was why most people fell off the sides of buildings when they tried to climb them. But Remo never fell off a building because he used gravity to push him forward, then redirected the momentum generated in his body by the gravity to push him upward.

It was the same with electricity. As he neared the top of the fence around the compound, he kept the palms of his hands and the soles of his feet exactly parallel to the surface of the fence, inches away from the steel frame. He kept in contact with the electric current, because that was what kept him suspended in air, but never varied his distance from the fence.

That control had taken him time to learn. At first,

during his practice sessions, he'd come too near the fence, and the electricity had jolted him, causing his muscles to tense. Then he was fighting electricity, and it was all over. No one fights electricity and wins. That was what the old man said.

The old man's name was Chiun. He had been an old man when Remo first met him, and he had known him most of his adult life. When the electric current felt as if it were going to fry Remo alive, Chiun had told him to relax and accept it. If anyone else had told him to hang loose while a lethal charge of electricity coursed through his body, Remo would have had words with the person. But Chiun wasn't just anyone. He was Remo's trainer. He had come into Remo's life to create, from the expired form of a dead police officer, a fighting machine more perfect than anything the Western world had ever known. Remo had been that policeman, framed for a crime he didn't commit, sentenced to die in an electric chair that didn't quite work.

Not quite. But bad enough. Years after the morning when he had come to in a room in Folcroft Sanitarium in Rye, New York, the burns still fresh on his wrists, he remembered that electric chair. Long after he'd met the lemon-faced man who had personally selected Remo for the experiment and introduced him to the ancient Korean trainer named Chiun, he remembered. A lifetime later, after Chiun had developed Remo's body into something so different from that of the normal human male that even his nervous system had changed, the fear of electricity still lurked inside Remo.

So when Chiun told him to relax, he was afraid. But he listened.

Now he made his way up the fence, the fringe-ends of the electric current in contact with his skin. His breathing was controlled and deep, his balance automatically adjusting with each small move. The current was the force that kept him aloft. Using it, never breaking contact, he slid slowly up the fence, moving his arms in slow circles to generate the friction that propelled him upward. At the top of the fence he broke suddenly, pulling his legs backward and over his head and somersaulting over the top.

The compound he was in was an acre or more of snow-covered gravel and frozen mud set in the far reaches of Staten Island. Rotting wooden crates, rusted cans, and soggy sheets of old newspapers littered the ground. At the rear of the compound stood a large, dirty cinderblock warehouse, six stories tall with a loading dock at the right end. A truck was parked at the loading dock. As Remo neared, he saw three burly men packing crates into the truck.

"Hi, guys," he said, thrusting his hand into a crate on the dock. He pulled out a five-pound bag of white powder encased in plastic. "Just as I thought," he said.

"Huh?" One of the dock workers pulled out a Browning .9mm automatic. "Who are you, mister?"

"I'm with the Heroin Control Board," Remo said through pursed lips. "I'm afraid this won't do. Sloppy packaging. No brand names. Not even a yellow plastic measuring spoon, like the coffee boys give out. No, this just isn't up to par. Sorry, boys." He yanked open the plastic bag and dumped its contents into the wind.

"Hey, that stuff's worth half a million dollars," the man with the Browning said.

"Do it right, or don't do it, that's our motto," Remo said.

"Move out of the way, fellas," the man holding the gun said two seconds before he fired. He was one second late. Because one second before he fired, Remo had coiled the barrel of the Browning into a corkscrew, and by the time the bullet left it, it was spinning toward the dock worker's chest, where it came to rest with a muffled *whump*.

"No gun, see?" another worker said, demonstrating his lack of weapons by raising his arms high in the air and wetting his pants.

"No gun, see?" the other said, falling to his knees, his hands clasped in front of him.

"You the boss?" Remo asked.

"No way," the worker said with touching sincerity. "We're just labor. Management's what you want, yessir."

"Who's management?"

"Mr. Bonelli. 'Bones' Bonelli. He's over there." He gestured wildly toward the interior of the warehouse.

Giuseppe "Bones" Bonelli sat behind a desk in the only carpeted and heated room in the place. Behind him was one small window, placed high above the floor. Seated in a huge red leather chair, he looked more like an overaged wraith than an underworld heroin don. His hair was thinning, and his leather skin fell in folds down his skull-like face, which was grinning in ecstasy. The top half of Giuseppe "Bones" Bonelli was a tiny, wrinkled, happy crone. The bottom half, displayed beneath the leg opening of the desk, was an ample, satin-covered rear end facing in the opposite direction. Below it protruded two spiky black high heels.

The satin oval swayed rhythmically. Bonelli's mouth opened to emit a small squeal of joy. "Oh. . . oh. . . shit," he said, noticing Remo standing in the doorway. "Who're you?"

One hand twitched frantically in his lap, while the

other pulled a ludicrously large Colt .45 from his jacket. "Arggh," he screamed, throwing the gun into the air. "Zipper. The freaking zipper's caught."

"Thanks," Remo said, grabbing the gun.

"Freaking zipper. It's all your fault."

"Use buttons," Remo said. "Or a fig leaf. In your case, maybe a grape leaf will do."

Bonelli's trigger finger moved back and forth several times before he noticed it was empty. "Gimme that gun."

"Sure," Remo said, crushing the Colt into dust and sifting it into Bonelli's open hand.

"Smart shit," Bonelli muttered. He kicked the girl under the desk. "Hey, you. Get outta here. I got business."

The satin oval wriggled out backwards and rose. It belonged to a statuesque blonde who carried the imprint of Bonelli's foot on her chest. "What about me?" she groused, her face contorted with anger. Then she saw Remo, and the anger disappeared.

Remo often had that effect on women. He saw her appraising eyes warm with approval as she took in the slender, taut body with the abnormally thick wrists, the well-muscled shoulders, the clean-shaven face accentuated by high cheekbones and long-lashed dark eyes, the thick black hair. She smiled.

"You come here often?" she asked.

"Only when I have to kill someone."

"You're cute."

"Get out of here!" Bonelli yelled. The girl sauntered away slowly, giving Remo the full benefit of her undulating posterior.

"What's this 'kill me' crap?" Bonelli spat. "What kind of talk is that?"

Remo shrugged. "That's what I'm here for."

"Oh, yeah?" With a quick motion, Bonelli yanked a knife out of his jacket and sliced the air with it. "Oh, yeah?"

"Yeah," Remo said, catching the knife by the blade. He tossed it upward in a spiral. The knife drilled a neat hole in the ceiling. Plaster dust sprinkled down on Bonelli's head and shoulders.

"Smart shit," Bonelli said. "Hey, what're you doing?"

"I'm taking you for a ride," Remo said, imitating all the gangsters he'd seen on late-night TV movies. He hoisted Bonelli over his shoulder.

"Watch it, creep. This here's a silk suit. Mess up my suit, I'm going to have to get serious with you."

Remo tore the pockets off the jacket. Two knives and a stiletto clanked out.

"Okay, buddy," Bonelli raged. "You asked for it now. Shorty! Shorty!"

"Shorty?" Remo guessed his cargo's weight at 110, tops. Bonelli was barely five feet tall. "Shorty? What's that make you, Paul Bunyan?"

Bonelli sneered. He jerked his thumb toward the window. "That's Shorty," he said.

The small overhead window was filled by a face. The face had little pig eyes and a nose so broken it looked like a ball of putty that had been run over by a tank tread. Soon the tops of two massive shoulders edged into the window. The pane burst in a shower of glass. Spiderweb cracks appeared in the window's corners and spread into the room, widening with thunderous claps. Then the wall gave and Shorty shot through the opening like a sausage with a lit fuse.

"You called, boss?"

"Yeah. Take care of this smart shit."

Shorty lumbered over to Remo. "This one?"

"Who else?" Bonelli roared. "There's you, me, and him in this room. You thinking about offing me?"

Shorty's face fell with humility. "Oh, no, boss. You're the boss. I wouldn't do that to you."

"Then you're maybe thinking about offing yourself?"

Shorty pondered for several moments, his brow furrowed in concentration. Then his forehead smoothed and he broke into a happy grin. "Oh. I get it. That's a joke, huh, boss? Off myself. That's funny, boss. Ha, ha."

"Shut up!"

"Okay, boss."

"Then who's that leave, Shorty?" Bonelli asked patiently.

Shorty looked around the room, counting on his fingers. 'Well, there's you. You ain't the one. And there's me. . . ha, ha, that was funny, boss."

"Who else, stupid?"

Shorty lumbered around until he faced Remo. "That leaves him," he said with conviction. He pulled back his oaken arm and blasted it forward.

"Right," said Bonelli.

"Wrong," said Remo. He flicked out two fingers to deflect the blow. Shorty's arm kept going, swinging around in a circle and finally landing in the middle of his own face, causing his oft-broken nose to disappear entirely. He fell forward with a deafening thud.

"So much for Shorty," Remo said as he lifted Bonelli again, this time by his belt, and carried him through the wrecked wall, dangling at his side.

"The belt, watch the belt," Bonelli said. "It's Pierre Cardin."

Remo began scaling the sheer wall of the warehouse. Bonelli looked down once and screamed. "Holy freaking shit," he yelled. "Where are you taking me?"

"Up." Remo climbed the wall methodically, his toes catching on the bricks of the building, his free hand gently guiding ahead and working with gravity to pull him upward.

"May the saints curse you," Giuseppe "Bones" Bonelli sobbed. "May your days be filled with suffering and hardship. May your mother's lasagne be laced with cow turds. May your children and your children's children—"

"Hey, zip it up, will you? I'm trying to kill somebody. You're wrecking my concentration."

"Always with the smart shit. May your grandchildren be smitten with boils. May your wife lie with lepers."

"Look, if you don't stop hurting my feelings, I'm going to forget about you and leave," Remo said.

"That's the idea. May your uncles choke on chicken bones."

"Just a second," Remo said, stopping. "Now that's getting personal. You don't mess with a guy's uncles. I'm leaving." He tossed Bonelli into the air. Bonelli shrieked, his voice growing small as he catapulted upwards.

"Take that back," Remo said.

"I take it back," Bonelli howled.

"How much?"

"All of it. Everything." He paused in midair for a moment, then began his screaming descent. "Help!"

"Will you shut up?"

"Yes. Yes. Forever. Silence."

"You'll let me concentrate?"

"Do anything you want. Jest catch me." As he approached eye-level with Remo, Remo reached out and clasped Bonelli by his belt. With a whoosh of air and frantic movements of a drowning man, Bonelli whinnied once, then opened his eyes a crack and discovered he was still alive.

"Smart—"

"Ah-ah-ah," Remo cautioned.

Bonelli was silent.

The rest of the six-story climb was peaceful. Remo whistled an ancient Korean tune he'd learned from Chiun. The melody was haunting and lovely, and the sound it made in the crisp winter air made it even more beautiful. In the background, birds were singing. Remo half forgot about the narcotics king dangling from his right arm as he made his way up the building.

Sometimes Remo almost enjoyed his job. He supposed that made him a pervert. Assassins weren't generally happy people, and Remo guessed that he was probably no happier than most people who killed other people for a living. But at least he killed people who deserved to be killed. He didn't hire himself out to greedy landlords who had stubborn tenants put away because those tenants didn't have the good grace to die quickly in their rent-controlled apartments. He didn't shoot foreign students because a thrill-crazed dictator decreed it. He killed when there was killing to be done. When there was nothing else that could be done.

Like all professional assassins, Remo did not decide whose souls would be liberated from their bodies. That was done for him by an organization developed by a president of the United States long ago as a lastditch emergency measure to control crime. Only the emergency never passed, and the president was himself murdered, and so the organization continued.

It was called CURE. CURE was possibly the most highly illegal instrument America had ever devised to combat crime. Unknown to all but three people on earth, CURE worked outside the Constitution—utterly outside. CURE had no rules, and only one objective: to control crime when every other method of controlling it had failed.

Of the three people who knew about CURE, the president of the United States was the least important. It was his option either to use the special red phone in a bedroom of the White House or not. The red phone was a direct line to CURE's headquarters in Rye, New York. Almost every president, upon learning from his predecessor about the red phone, swore that CURE would never be used. The existence of an organization like CURE was an admission that America's legal system had failed miserably, and no new president would admit that. And so the red phone would rest, forgotten, for months at a time at the beginning of each new administration. But eventually it was used. It was always used.

And when that red-phone was picked up, it was answered immediately by a lemony-voiced man, the second person who knew of CURE's existence. That man was Dr. Harold W. Smith.

Smith was as unlikely a personality to run an illegal organization as could be found on the face of the earth. His principal interest lay in computer information analysis. He was precise, fastidious, methodical, and law-abiding by nature.

His job, as director of CURE, brought him into daily contact with murder, arson, treason, blackmail, and other forms of man-made catastrophe. The long-dead president who had begun CURE had hand-picked Smith, knowing that illegal work would be difficult for him. Smith had been chosen because he possessed one quality, which the president knew would override all possible objections Smith could have about the nature of his work: Harold W. Smith loved his country more than anything else. He would see to it that the job got done. Or didn't get done, according to the best interests of the country. Even the president himself could do no more than suggest assignments to Harold W. Smith. CURE obeyed no one.

The third person who knew about CURE was the enforcement arm of the organization. One man, trained in an ancient form of defense and attack developed millennia ago in the small Korean village of Sinanju. One man who could perform the impossible.

That man was Remo Williams.

He had scaled all six stories of the warehouse now, the silent but pained-looking Giuseppe "Bones" Bonelli in tow. Below, the two dock workers were once again loading the crates full of white death into the parked truck. As he tossed Bonelli onto the flat, snow-covered roof, the small man grimaced and clutched at his side.

"What's the matter?" Remo asked dubiously.

"It's just that song."

"What song?"

"The one you kept whistling. You know, over and over, over and over."

"What about it?"

Bonelli doubled over. "It gave me gas," he said. "I didn't want to say nothing over there"—he gestured vaguely over the side—"but, I mean, like if you've got to sing, couldn't you do 'My Way' or 'I Left My Heart in San Francisco'?" Not that weird shit. Gives me a pocket, right here." He pointed to a region of his intestines.

"You've just got no taste," Remo said. Chiun was getting to him, he knew. He was even beginning to remind himself of Chiun.

But he wouldn't worry about that, he decided. He wouldn't worry because at the moment there were other things to worry about. Like the fact that Giuseppe "Bones" Bonelli had reached into his inside coat pocket and was unfolding something metallic with a black handle. It was a hatchet. Chortling with glee, Bonelli swung it in Remo's direction, the blade singing.

"Okay, smart shit. You asked for it." He brought the blade home. It struck at exactly the place where Remo's head was, only Remo's head was no longer there. The thin young man had miraculously moved to another spot in a movement so fast that Bonelli couldn't follow it. Bonelli struck again. And missed.

"I wish you'd cut this out," Remo said, casually tossing the hatchet away. In the distance, outside the compound, it buried itself deep in a large tree.

"Nice," Bonelli said admiringly. "Hey, who are you, anyway?"

"Call me Remo."

Bonelli smiled broadly. "Remo. That's a nice name, sonny. Sounds Italian. You Italian?"

"Maybe," Remo said. He was an orphan. As far as he knew, his ancestry could have been anything.

"I thought so. You got a brain like a *paisan*. That was good, that tree. Say, Remo, I could use a guy like you in the business."

"I don't think I like your business."

"Hey, it's good money. And you'll be part of the family. Do lots of family things together."

"Like shooting dope into children."

"Remo, *paisan*," he said expansively. "It's business, that's all. Supply and demand. Buy low, sell high. I'll show you all the ropes."

Remo thought about it. "No, I don't think so," he said. "There's something else I'd rather do."

"More than making money? Come on."

"No," Remo protested. "I really think I'd rather do this other thing."

"What's that?"

"I'd rather kill you."

Bonelli snarled. "Okay, kid. You had your chance. No more Mister Nice Guy." He rifled through his trouser pockets and pulled out a grenade. "You leave now, or I pull the plug."

"Like this?" Remo said, snatching it away from him and pulling out the pin.

"What'd you do that for? Throw it, quick."

Remo tossed the grenade up in the air absently and caught it behind his back. "Nah," he said. "I'm tired of throwing." He tossed it up in the air again. Bonelli leaped up, but Remo caught it just above Bonelli's reach.

"Give me that."

"What for?" Remo asked, juggling the grenade in one hand.

"I'll throw it," Bonelli said, sweat pouring down his face.

"I've got a better idea," Remo said. "You eat it." He stuffed the grenade into Bonelli's mouth and shook his hand. "Nice to meet you. I'll keep your offer in mind."

Then he flipped Bonelli into the air and the man fell, eyes bulging, on a direct course with the truck below. The crates had all been loaded. The back of the truck was sealed, and the two workers were sitting in the cab up front, its motor running.

Good timing, Remo thought as Giuseppe "Bones" Bonelli landed on top of the truck and blew to fragments.

For a moment, the air was filled with a miasma of white powder containing shards of splintered wood. Then the sky was clear again, and blue and cold, and Remo climbed down the building, singing an old Korean tune.

Chiun was singing the same tune when Remo walked into the Manhattan motel room they shared. The lyrics, translated from the Korean, went something like: "O lovely one, when I behold your gracious ways, your beauty, like the melting snow of spring, makes my heart weep with tears of joy." He was singing it while gazing at himself in the mirror, arranging the folds of his gold brocade robe. He swayed as he sang, causing the white wisps of hair on his head and chin to move softly. In the background, the television blared a commercial, in which a foul-tempered ten-year-old girl refused to let her younger brother use the family's coveted toothpaste, while her mother smiled on benignly.

"What is this racket?" Remo said, switching off the television.

"Lout," Chiun muttered. He jumped off the dresser, where he had been sitting, and seemed to float to the ground. "Who can expect a white man to appreciate beauty?" He turned the television on again. "O lovely one, when I behold your gracious ways. . ."

"Look, Little Father, if you're going to sing, don't you think it'll be less distracting without the TV?"

"Only a pale piece of pig's ear can be so easily distracted. Besides, there is nothing worth watching on the television."

"Then why do you have it on?"

Chiun sighed exasperatedly. "I have it on because there is going to be something worth watching. Anyone can see that."

The screen now showed a boxy, cheaply constructed compact automobile racing down a hill to the accompaniment of an orchestra.

"What?" Remo shouted above the din of the *William Tell Overture*.

The automobile drove off the screen and was replaced by the venomous stare of an Oriental newswoman who looked as if she ate babies for breakfast.

"Oh, it is she," Chiun said breathlessly, his long-nailed hands fluttering to his chest as he drifted into a lotus position in front of the set.

"This is Cheeta Ching welcoming you to the WACK NEWS UPDATE," she snarled. "It's really bad news tonight," she added, her flat features twisting into a malevolent grin.

"O lovely one. O gracious person," Chiun rhapsodized.

"Oh, cut me a break," Remo said. "*This* is what's worth watching? This vicious harpy?"

"Out," Chiun commanded. "You do not deserve to be in the same room as the beautiful lotus blossom Miss Cheeta Ching. You who prefer the cowlike teats of Western giantesses. You who prefer the vacuous stares of round-eyed, white-skinned fools like yourself."

"I, who prefer just about anything to Cheeta

Ching," Remo said. As he left the room, Cheeta was spewing out the terrible events of the day with grisly delight.

"Police have still not identified the participants in the grotesque murder of Secretary of the Air Force Homer G. Watson, known to Third World circles as a warmongering capitalist pig. Watson was executed in his home early yesterday by one or more assailants using what might have been a flame thrower, police report. The flame thrower theory was based on localized fire damage in the victim's Maryland home. Watson's charred and mutilated corpse was identified through dental records. Police report that everything possible is being done to locate the perpetrators of the murder, but so far, no clues are available. As a final note, we at WACK salute the valiant freedom fighters who so efficiently eliminated the Air Force bureaucrat with a hearty 'Well done, boys.' "

"Oh, Mr. Remo," the girl at the motel's reception desk called crisply. "There's a message for you." She picked a neatly folded piece of paper out of Remo's room slot. "Call Aunt Mildred," she read primly. "That is all the message says. You are to call Aunt Mildred."

"Smitty's back to Aunt Mildred again," Remo mumbled.

The girl clapped her hands over her ears. "We are not concerned with the private lives of our guests, Mr. Remo."

"Fine. Do you have a pay phone here?"

"You have a phone in your room, Mr. Remo."

"I know. I'm not allowed in there."

"I told you, we are not interested in the private lives of our guests. Why don't you use the phone in your room?"

"I don't want to use the phone in my room. I want to

use a pay phone. Now tell me where the pay phone is."

"Oh, all right." She pointed an icy finger down the hall.

As Remo turned the corner, he saw her scurry to the switchboard and rearrange the wiring on it. He walked into the phone booth and lifted the receiver. As he had expected, the faint sound of breathing emanated from the other end, where the girl was listening in.

He pitched his voice low. "In five seconds I'm going to grab that pretty woman at the switchboard and tear all her clothes off," he rumbled.

There was a little shriek from the other end before the line went dead. The receptionist's skirt billowed in the wind as she ran out the door.

Remo caught her before she hit the sidewalk. "Okay, what's the idea?"

"I—I don't know what you're talking about," she said. "Are you really going to tear all my clothes off?"

"You were listening in on my phone call. Who do you work for?"

"Nobody."

"Who?" He grasped her hand more tightly.

"Okay, okay," she said testily. "It doesn't matter, I suppose."

"Who is it?"

"I don't know. That's the truth. Somebody called me and asked me to monitor all the phone lines. The ones in the rooms are easier, but I can get the pay-phones, too, with a little switch on the wires."

"What for?"

"Who knows? He just wanted me to write down anything anybody said about the army, the navy, or the air force. I get twenty dollars for every item I send in to the computer information center in Albuquerque."

"Computers?" Remo asked, raising an eyebrow.

"Yes. He said I'd get a government check. I figured he was from the CIA or the FBI or something like that."

"What did this guy sound like?"

"Sound? Well, kind of—lemony, I guess. That's the only way to describe it. Sort of like your Aunt Mildred."

"All right," Remo said with disgust. Smith had struck again. For an operation as minuscule in size as CURE, Smith had tentacles reaching into every corner of every city in the world. "Forget it. I didn't mean to scare you." He walked down the street.

"Hey, wait a minute," the girl called after him. Her face was a caricature of disappointment. "Aren't you going to rip off my clothes now?"

"Later," Remo said.

He found a pay phone down the street and dialed the Chicago Dial-a-Prayer number that connected automatically with Smith's phone at Folcroft Sanitarium. "Yes?" came Smith's acid voice.

"What in hell are you doing now?"

"Meet me in one hour on Mott Street in Chinatown," Smith said.

"I want to know why you have henchmen listening in on my phone calls at the E-Z Rest Motel."

"Not yours, Remo. Everyone's. That person is one of thousands who've been contacted."

"What's going on?"

"I'll fill you in later. One hour. The dragon." Smith hung up.

There was only one dragon in Chinatown, and that was the one winding its way down Mott Street in the Chinese New Year's parade.

"Excuse me," Remo said, pressing his way through the crush of cheering spectators.

"It is everywhere," Chiun said ominously behind him.

Remo looked around. "What's everywhere?"

"Pork," the old man said. "The smell of stir-fried pork is emanating from every barbaric Chinese mouth here."

"Take it easy."

"Only a white man would ask a Korean to tolerate a mob of pork-eating Chinese."

"Then why did you come along? You didn't have to come to Chinatown," Remo said irritably.

Chiun sniffed. "I came because it is my duty to come," he said archly. "As the Master of Sinanju, it is imperative that I attend to Emperor Smith's wishes personally."

"Little Father, I work for Smitty. You're my trainer. You don't have to come."

"I do," Chiun insisted. "When the Emperor wishes to bestow a gift upon a valued assassin, the receiver of that gift should be present. It is only polite."

"Gift? What gift?"

"The portrait of Cheeta Ching. Emperor Smith has promised it to me."

"You already have a portrait of that flat-nosed barracuda. You've made a shrine out of it."

"That portrait is of Cheeta Ching in Western dress. I requested one of the beautiful and gracious lady attired in the traditional robes of her native Korea."

"She doesn't even know where Korea is. For her, the underside of one rock's as good as another."

"White lout. Pork eater."

"I thought the Chinese were the pork eaters of the day."

"Chinese, white, what difference does it make? A waste is a waste."

As they neared the multicolored paper-maché dragon, it began to wobble and stagger randomly down the street, knocking over a fried-noodle stand. Remo slid under the cloth sides of the beast in time to see Smith buckle in exhaustion to the ground. He picked Smith up with one arm while supporting the sweltering shell of the dragon with the other.

"You okay, Smitty?"

"You're fourteen minutes late," Smith said, consulting his Timex. "How long did you think I could hold this thing up by myself?"

"Sorry, Smitty." He set him on his feet. "Why are we meeting here, anyway?"

"Silence, brainless one," Chiun said. "The Emperor has chosen to meet us in this teeming, stinking location because he is a man of great sensitivity and humility." He bowed to Smith. "He wishes to bestow his gift of beauty in the midst of squalor to demonstrate that loveliness can transcend all ugliness. Oh, very wise, Emperor. Most fitting."

"I'm not an emperor, Chiun," Smith began to explain for the hundredth time. Chiun persisted in believing that Smith had hired Remo and Chiun for the same reasons emperors throughout history had hired Chiun's ancestors. "Oh, never mind," Smith said.

"I am honored to accept your gift, O mighty one," Chiun said, smiling.

"Gift?" Smith looked to Remo. "What gift?"

"A picture of the Korean version of Godzilla in drag," Remo said.

"The photograph," Chiun prompted. "The portrait of the beauteous Cheeta Ching."

"I thought I got one of those for you."

"In ceremonial robes. The traditional Maiden's Portrait." His wrinkled face was falling in disappointment. "You have not forgotten?"

"Er, I'm afraid I have," Smith said impatiently. "I'll see what I can do. I've brought you here because what I have to tell you is of the utmost secrecy—and must remain so."

"Like the requests of your valued assassins," Chiun muttered.

"I beg your pardon?"

"Never mind," Remo said. "Go on."

Smith spoke urgently. "You know, perhaps, that the Secretary of the Air Force was murdered yesterday morning."

"I think I heard part of that. Burned by a flame-thrower or something."

"Right. What the press doesn't know is that last night the Secretary of the Navy, Thornton Ives, was murdered, too. Bayonetted. He was ambushed outside the home of Senator John Spangler in Virginia. It looks like the work of more than one assassin."

"A white assassin," Chiun grumbled. "Only a white man would attempt to kill with a net. For a real assassin, one comes to the Master of Sinanju. But does one bother to honor the small request of the aging Master? Never. Perhaps we should use nets, too. We could bludgeon the enemy with the holes."

"A bayonet isn't a net, Little Father," Remo explained. "It's a sort of spear on the end of a rifle."

"Oh, I see. The white assassin uses a rifle to stab with. Very efficient."

"Get off the snot, Chiun," Remo said in Korean. "Just because you didn't get your picture."

"Just because the one small light in my twilit years has been extinguished. . . ."

"Please, please," Smith said. "We have limited time."

"Forgive me, O Emperor," Chiun said with humility. "I will not speak again. Who cares to hear the pleas of an old man, anyway?"

"Now really—" Smith began, but Chiun clamped his jaws together and turned his back. Smith sighed and went on. "The man who found the body, a gardener at the Spangler house, doesn't know anything. The FBI and the CIA have been grilling him ever since he reported the incident."

"To the police?"

"No. The police are being kept out of this. They've lost every lead on the murder of the Secretary of the Air Force, and the president is afraid they'll bungle this one, too. We can't afford that. It's beginning to look like a pattern."

"Who's next?"

"The Secretary of the Army, probably. The Secret Service already has a twenty-four-hour guard on him, as well as on key persons around the president. But it can't go on indefinitely. Whoever is carrying out these killings has to be stopped."

"Is that why you've got your spy network going full tilt?"

"Of course. Since we have nothing, any scrap of information may help to bring some pieces of the puzzle to light."

"Okay," Remo said. "If these guys were killed by flame-throwers and bayonets, it could be the work of the military. Want me to start there?"

"I don't think so. All the branches of the military are carrying out their own investigations, and I'm already tapped into their computer information banks. I think you ought to start at the scene of the crime. Go to Senator Spangler's house and see who else was at the party last night. The guests there were the last to see Admiral Ives alive."

"That's routine police work," Remo protested.

"We have every reason to believe this isn't a routine murder," Smith said. "And we have to start somewhere. All the police know is that a body was found on the front lawn of the Spangler residence. The senator's daughter, Cecilia, alerted the FBI immediately, and the body was removed from the morgue before it was identified."

"Then why doesn't the FBI handle this?"

Smith checked his watch. "Remo, if we had two years, the FBI could handle it. But we don't. The heads of two military branches of the United States government have been eliminated, and I don't know if we've seen the end of this spree. The president is alarmed. We have to work fast, before things get worse."

"All right, all right," Remo said, not relishing the idea of slogging around, asking questions of every guest at a drunken Washington party. "But I don't see where it's going to get us."

"It will get us out of this stinking pork hole," Chiun said in Korean. "Say yes. Pretend the emperor knows what he's talking about. Then we can return to civilization."

"I thought you weren't speaking."

"I am not speaking to him. To you, I speak. Take me home."

"To the land of the round eyes?"

"To the television," Chiun snapped. "Miss Ching's news brief will be broadcasting soon."

"Oh," Remo said. "Look, Smitty, I think we ought to discuss this some more."

Someone was pounding violently on the sides of the dragon and screaming in Chinese. Then a head peered inside, waving a ten-dollar bill and pointing at his watch.

"I think our time's up," Smith said. "I rented this thing for a half-hour."

"For ten bucks," Remo said. "No wonder you brought us here. It was cheaper than a cab."

"Ten dollars is sufficient payment," Smith said acidly.

"You know, Smitty, you're really a cheapskate."

"That is no concern of yours."

Chiun bowed and slipped out of the papier-mâché dragon. In another moment, the Chinese man who was screaming at Smith disappeared. Remo pulled up the cloth covering and saw Chiun in the crowd, speaking and gesturing loftily to the Chinese, who bowed and nodded in understanding. Then Chiun returned and bowed once before Smith.

"We will take our leave now, O illustrious Emperor, and leave you to your peace. Do not waste a moment's thought on my humble request for a picture of the beautiful lady. It means nothing to anyone but myself, and my lowly needs do not concern one so mighty as you. Come, Remo."

As they left, a crowd of Chinese stripped the dragon off Smith and clambered around him, shouting angrily.

"What's with them?" Remo asked. Smith was looking around helplessly in the center of the noisy mob.

"They feel the Emperor has cheated them," Chiun said.

"I wonder who gave them that idea."

Chiun shrugged. "It was not I. I would never betray the Emperor who pays the pittance to my village for the services of the Master of Sinanju.''

"I saw you talking to that guy. What did you say?''

"I told him only that the last time I hired the use of one of those cloth and paper beasts, I paid the sum of one hundred dollars. Anything below that would be a grave insult. That is what I told him."

Remo saw Smith finally take out his wallet and hand a small wad of bills to the Chinese man. The Chinese bowed, and Smith awkwardly bowed back, glaring angrily at Remo and Chiun.

"I think we'd better get out of town for a while,'' Remo said.

Chapter Three

The Virginia residence of Senator John Spangler was a sprawling, plantation-style mansion surrounded by snow-tipped gardens and white pillars. A fat, middle-aged woman in dungarees and a sweat shirt opened the door before Remo knocked. "If you're from the press, get out of here," she said.

"Is this the Spangler house?"

"You know it is. Scram."

"You're not Mrs. Spangler, are you?"

"No." She slammed the door. Remo stopped it with his pinky. The door shuddered and loosened on its hinges.

"Is she at home?" Remo asked politely.

"What do you think you're doing?" the woman yelled above the whistling wind as she lunged toward the door, which began to fall into the room.

He entered through the huge black and white tiled anteroom into a grand and spacious sitting room. Above the mantle hung a portrait of the senator, a vigorous, youngish man in the bloom of life. In the distance he heard a woman's voice shrieking.

"I told you to hang the Bob Mackie dresses, not pack them," the voice raged. "That bag's for cookies.

Don't drop it. One broken cookie and it's curtains, understand?''

"Yes, mum," a deferential man's voice said.

"The last servant who dropped my cookie bag is doing time in Leavenworth."

"Yes, mum." The man spoke as he descended a curving staircase, carrying six pieces of luggage. The three people behind him were hefting several bags apiece as well. The entourage lumbered through the large entrance.

Behind them, swathed in a long sable coat, was a beautiful brunette stuffing cookies into her mouth. On her head she was wearing a turban covered with violet flowers to match her eyes.

Apparently oblivious to Remo, she squinted meanly at the sight of the fat lady who was puffing as she tried to right the door into its frame. "What have you broken now?" she snapped.

The fat lady turned around, her expression one of deep hurt. "I didn't do anything," she explained. "It was him." She pointed to Remo. "He barged in here—"

"Well, well," the violet-eyed brunette said, suddenly flashing a dazzling smile at Remo. "It's been a long time, darling."

"We've never met," Remo said. "Are you Mrs. Spangler?"

She stared at him blankly. "I don't remember," she said. "I'm Mrs. Somebody. I always am. My husband's name is Paul. Or George. Something ordinary." She pointed to the portrait of the senator on top of the mantle. "John,—that's it. See, up there above the fireplace? That's my husband. I think. Unless the divorce came through. Are you my lawyer?"

"No," Remo said. "I'm a friend of a friend."

"You're lovely. What's your name?" She gobbled down another cookie.

"Remo."

She pondered. "Remo. I've never been married to a Remo before. Unless it was an awfully long time ago. We've never been married, have we, Remo?"

"I don't think so."

"Wonderful. I have a simply divine wedding gown I've been saving. Would next Thursday be all right?"

"I think I'll be too busy to get married," Remo said.

"Pity. Well, I have to be off. Toodle-oo."

"I'd like to ask you a few questions before you go. About the party."

"Party? Was it a wedding?"

"I don't think so."

"Good. I was just beginning to get used to what's-his-name."

"The senator?"

"Yes, that's him. I was married to him once."

"I thought you were married to him now."

"Am I? How marvelous. George is such a dear."

"John," the fat lady corrected.

"John? Did I actually marry John?"

"John Spangler," Remo said. "The senator."

She burst into peals of laughter. "But that's too divine! I married the senator. Wait until my friends hear about it. Here, have a cookie." She offered the bag to Remo. "Not a big one. The big ones are for me. Just wet your finger and stick it to a few crumbs."

"I'll pass," Remo said. "Mrs. Spangler, I'd really like to talk to you about Thornton Ives, the Secretary of the Navy. He was a guest at your party last night."

"Now you're wasting your time," she said firmly.

"Whoever this Thornton Ives is, he's no husband of mine. I would never marry a secretary. What kind of diamonds can a secretary afford?"

"He was the Secretary of the Navy. An admiral or something."

"Oh," she said. "That's different. I do love shipboard romances. Has he sent you to ask for my hand?"

"He's dead, ma'am. Somebody murdered him last night outside this house. With a bayonet."

"What a shame," Mrs. Spangler sighed. "A honeymoon on board a yacht would have been divine. Charles and Di adored theirs. Now do be off, my dear. There's a good boy," she said, shuffling Remo out the door. "If I miss my plane, I'll be absolutely brokenhearted. Such a bother, traveling to airports like this. My third husband—or maybe it was the sixth—had his own plane. I should have stayed with him. Ralph was so sweet. I mean Richard. I'm sure it was Richard. He gave me a lovely diamond for our one-week wedding anniversary. Well, no matter." She patted Remo on the shoulder. "Do stay in touch, darling. It was divine while it lasted. I'll never love another man like you again." She kissed him briefly on his cheek and brushed past the fat lady without a word on her way to the waiting limo. A moment later the car was whooshing down the curving drive.

Remo stood in silence. It was broken shortly by rude laughter. The fat lady beside him pressed the door back into place with a final whack, her sides shaking with mirth.

"Very funny," Remo said.

"I can tell you've never been here before. Hoo."

"Hoo, yourself. Who else is around?"

"No one. Just me."

"The senator?"

"He's already at the farm. Mother's gone to join him."

"Mother?" Remo asked. "Who's mother?"

"The dizzy broad who just left. That's Mama. Mater. Mommie Dearest. Mammy. The vine which has yielded the tender grape standing before you. Me."

Remo looked at the woman incredulously. She was easily twice the age of the cookie-eating doll who got into the limo. "You mean she's your stepmother or something," Remo said.

"My real mother, Bozo," she shouted. She scraped some dried egg off her coveralls with a filthy thumbnail. "I guess I don't look much like a senator's daughter," she said more somberly.

"Look," Remo said. "You can be anybody's daughter you want to be." The world was full of hooples. "Just tell me where I can find—this person—Cecilia Spangler."

"Quit treating me like a fruitcake," she said, her hands resting on her vast hips. "The Spanglers have one daughter, and that's Cecilia, and that's me. But I don't care if you want to talk to me or not, because I'm not going to talk to you. So make like an egg and beat it."

Just then a black maid stepped into the vestibule. "Telephone for you, Miss Spangler."

"Tell whoever it is I'm busy. Tell them I'm dead. I don't care. Neither will they."

"Yes, Miss."

"Probably some charity looking for money. Nobody else calls me," she said.

Remo looked back at the retreating figure of the maid. "Are you really Cecilia Spangler?"

"I told you who I was. Which is more than you've done. Remo who?"

"Remo Williams. A friend of a friend."

"Friend of whose?"

"Of yours," Remo lied.

"Can it, reporter. I don't have friends who have friends who look like you. Only mother has those friends. And they're all at the same place she is."

"Where's that?"

"Some fat farm or something," Cecilia said, waving the thought away. "She goes there every month. She claims that's how she and daddy stay so young. Big deal. I don't care how she looks. I don't care how I look. I know I'm a pig, and I don't care, see?" Her teeth were bared.

"Fine," Remo said placatingly. "You don't have to get nasty."

"Of course I have to get nasty. Wouldn't you be nasty if your mother looked like your daughter and you looked like everybody's fat maiden aunt?"

"I wouldn't know," Remo said. "I never thought about it." He tweaked her left earlobe. It was one of the 52 steps to sexual ecstasy Chiun had taught him. If anything made women talk, the left earlobe did it. "I'm not a reporter," he said softly, feeling her squirm beneath his touch. "But I've got to ask you some questions about the murder on your lawn last night."

"That feels wonderful," she said, shivering.

"The guy who got killed was the Secretary of the Navy. Did you know that?" He moved slowly toward the inside of her elbows. In the teachings of Sinanju, the rigid sequence of steps had to be followed precisely. Each step slowly aroused the woman to the heights of physical pleasure, until she was broken and consumed and satisfied.

Remo had pleasured many women for many purposes. Not all of the women had been desirable, and his purposes were rarely spurred by his own desire. But women always performed the way he expected them to under the guidance of his skillful hands. They took the pleasure he gave them, and in return they offered him whatever he needed—information, time, complicity.

He hated it. Love was never a question. Neither was pleasure, for Remo. He had ceased deriving pleasure from the act long ago. It was just part of his job, along with watching women like Cecilia Spangler—hurt, long forgotten, ugly girls who were never touched with sincerity or affection and knew it and didn't care any more. Remo felt dirty.

"Of course I knew who he was. I was the one who called the FBI. Everybody else was too drunk. What are you doing to my elbow?"

"Tell me what you know about him. Ives. The Secretary of the Navy." Get it over with, he thought.

"Thornton Ives," she said quietly. "He was a nice man. . . . He was old. He let himself get old. I liked that." A tear welled up in one eye and rolled down the side of her face. "Please," she said. "Please stop that."

Remo was genuinely surprised. "Why? Don't you like it?"

"Oh, I like it all right," she said. "But sooner or later you'll find out that I don't know anything, and then you'll get mad and call me a fat pig. That's what reporters usually do with me."

"I told you, I'm not a reporter," Remo said, exasperated. He took her hand. "And I wouldn't do that to you."

She squeezed her eyes shut. "I don't know anything about the murder. I don't know who, I don't know why, I don't know anything except where, because it was in my front yard, and I wanted to keep things quiet because Admiral Ives was the only one of Mother's and Daddy's friends who didn't treat me like I was an embarrassment to the family." She stood up and paced around the room, looking like a miserable, shaggy farm animal.

"I was never even invited to their parties, here in my own house. Mother was so afraid somebody would take a look at me and figure out that she's fifty-eight years old. But Admiral Ives didn't care. He could have stayed young. He had the money. But he didn't. He was normal. He was the only normal person who ever came to this zoo."

She turned to Remo in a rage. "So don't waste your time seducing me. It won't be worth it."

"You're pretty sharp, aren't you?"

She sat down next to him, her red-rimmed eyes sullen. Slowly they kindled with the beginnings of a smile. "It was a pretty ridiculous pretense, acting like you wanted me."

"I'm sorry, Cecilia," Remo said.

"It's all right. It's been done before. And my pride isn't holding me back or anything." She laughed softly. "What pride? I'll take anything I can get, usually. But not over this. Thornton Ives was worth more to me than a quick feel. Although I must say you're awfully good at it."

Remo smiled.

"You think I'm crazy, don't you?"

"No," he said softly. "I don't. I think you're less crazy than your mother, for what that's worth. And I think you have more pride than you give yourself credit for."

Cecilia blew her nose into a used Kleenex from her pocket. "You're all right, too. Too bad you're a reporter."

"Once and for all, I'm not a reporter. I can't tell you who I work for. All I can say is that there are no police on this case, so if you don't help me out, we're all going to lose a lot of time. It's too bad that Ives is dead, but we're dealing with more than just one murder."

"Two," Cecilia said. "The Secretary of the Air Force bought the farm yesterday."

"Okay. And you didn't call the FBI instead of the cops just because you forgot the precinct phone number."

She looked at Remo for a long moment. "You really on our side?" she asked.

"I am. Will you help me?"

She shrugged. "If I can. What do you want?"

"A guest list. From the party last night."

"There's one in the library. I'll get it for you."

The list contained more than a hundred names. "Any idea where I should start?"

"It won't take long. Most of the people on that list won't be at home, anyway. They're all over at the fat farm with Mother and Daddy."

"Where's that?"

"I couldn't tell you. I was never invited there. It's not important, anyway. Just some clinic in Pennsylvania, like the ones in Switzerland, only closer. Mud baths, tonic, carrots for dinner, that kind of thing. That's what Mother tells me, anyway."

"And the others? Would anyone especially want to kill Admiral Ives?"

"Sure," Cecilia said. "The Russians, the Libyans, the PLO, the Red Brigades, the Baader Meinhof, the Red Chinese, you name it. He was the secretary of the navy, you know."

"You can drop the sarcasm," Remo said. "I get enough of that at home."

"Oh? You got a mother, too?"

"You might say that."

She showed him to the door and swung it open with a grunt. "Thanks," Remo said. "If I kissed you good-bye, would you get upset?"

She smiled. "Try me."

He touched her lips lightly. She blushed. "I don't suppose you'd like to start with the left earlobe again," she said.

Chapter Four

The first eighteen names on the Spangler's guest list were out of town. Since he'd exhausted the Washington, Virginia, and Maryland numbers, Remo went on to the New York City addresses.

Number nineteen was Bobby Jay, a name Remo recalled from years of listening to Chiun's television blasting while Remo was doing his exercises. Bobby Jay, according to his TV commercials, was one of the world's outstanding voices, known so far only to the discerning tastes of Europeans, but now available to Americans through a special TV offer. His records, according to the announcer, were not sold in stores, a fact gratefully acknowledged by millions, since Bobby Jay was, to all intents and purposes, tone deaf.

Back from a recent engagement at Phil's Steak House in Atlantic City, Bobby Jay himself answered the door in the Manhattan penthouse apartment. He was around thirty, with coiffed hair and the kind of boyish, unlined face that bespoke a lifetime of fighting off anything resembling intelligent thought.

"Hey, good-lookin', what you got cookin'?" he crooned tunelessly in greeting, snapping his fingers off the beat.

From the décor of the room, which consisted of sculpture, paintings, needlepoint, and other media depicting the backsides of naked man, Remo got the distinct impression that Bobby Jay was going to burst into a torrent of lisping in a matter of seconds.

He was right.

"Honey, are you the ethcort?"

"I'm the stranger," Remo said. "And I'd like to keep it that way."

Bobby Jay's eyes scanned the physique of the young man who stood in front of him, wearing chinos and a black T-shirt. "You mean you're not here to drive me to the airport?" he asked.

"Don't tell me you're leaving town, too."

"Everybody who's anybody is, darling. Oh, pooh. Where is that boy? I'm so annoyed I could spit." The lisp had changed to a slight whistle. He plopped down on a gigantic white sofa bordered with freshly cut calla lilies. "Come and sit down beside me. You'll make me feel better."

"Buddy, if I end up on that sofa next to you, I can guarantee you won't feel better."

"Well, I never. Who are you, anyway? Some kind of burglar or something? In that cute little T-shirt? It's January, macho man."

"I'm not a burglar. I want to ask you some questions about the party last night."

"Who, Elwood? That was nothing. It was just one of those things. . ." he sang.

"The party at the Spanglers."

". . .Just one of those fabulous flings. . ."

Remo clapped Bobby Jay's arm behind him in a hammerlock.

"Oh, you big brute," Bobby said, batting his eyelashes.

"I don't want singing. I want talking."

"Gawd, so intense. And what nice wrists you have. So thick and naughty. Well. What do you want to talk about, brown eyes? Would you like to hear about my rise to stardom? I was an overnight success, you might say, in the literal sense."

"I want to talk about Admiral Thornton Ives, the Secretary of the Navy. Did you know him?"

Bobby Jay giggled. "Not in the Biblical sense."

Remo collared him. "If you don't start giving me some straight answers, I'm going to punch you out. In the unconscious sense."

"I love it when you play rough."

Remo counted to ten. "Okay. Let's start over. What was your relationship with Admiral Ives?"

"Ugh, please. That old man? I'd never have a relationship with a sixty-year-old sailor. What do you think I am, a tart? I'd rather drown in a sea of elephant piss. Say, I never thought about that before. Sounds kind of kinky—elephant piss. What do you think?"

"I think you'd have a swell time. Were you friends with the admiral?"

"God, no. He wasn't part of the group."

"What group?"

Bobby Jay smiled lewdly and sidled closer to Remo. "Why, the *in* group, of course. The jet-setters. The beau monde. The BPs. All the people who matter."

"Like who?"

"Oh, everyone. Mrs. Spangler and the senator, they're part of the group. And Posie Ponselle, the actress—"

"Posie Ponselle? I thought she was dead."

"Oh, stars, no. Posie's still lovely. For a woman. Although she must be a hundred years old by now," he added maliciously. "But that's Shangri-la for you.

Oops, I suppose I shouldn't have said that. It's so hard to keep a secret from the man of your dreams.''

"Shangri-la?"

"Yeah. You know, 'Your kisses take me . . .' ''

"I know the tune, thanks," Remo said.

Bobby Jay stroked his arm. "It's a health clinic."

"In Pennsylvania?"

"Yes. Have you been there?"

"No," Remo said. "That's where Mrs. Spangler was going when I talked to her. What about it?"

"Now, I really can't say any more. They'll all just be boiling if they find out I've told an outsider about us. You do understand, don't you? If everybody knew about Shangri-la, all the fat paupers in the world would be storming the place."

"Sure," Remo said. "Wouldn't want to get a bad element in there with the likes of you and the other BMs."

"BPs," Bobby corrected. "That stands for Beautiful People." He pressed close to Remo.

"Think you'd qualify as a Beautiful Person with two black eyes and a broken nose?"

Bobby Jay moved away, sniffing scornfully. "Philistine. And I was going to ask you if you wanted to join. Not that you could anyway. I can tell you're not rich enough. Your T-shirt doesn't even have anybody's name on it."

Remo pulled out the guest list Cecilia Spangler had given him. Posie Ponselle's name was one of the people Remo had tried to reach. She was out of town. "Will you look at these names?" he asked Bobby Jay, indicating the first section of his list. Bobby did, and handed it back.

"Yes?"

"You said that the senator and Mrs. Spangler were

on their way to this Shangri-la place. Apparently, Posie Ponselle made the same trip, and you're going there, too. Are any of the other names on this list members of your club?"

"But of course, gorgeous. Most of them."

"Where is this place?"

"Ah, ah. I told you, I can't reveal any more. Unless you're thinking of joining."

"Then let's say I am."

Bobby Jay chuckled. "It's not so easy. The application fee is three thousand dollars, and you have to make at least a half-million a year."

"A half-million? How'd you get in?"

"My roommate's a tax lawyer," Bobby said.

"Pretty fancy club. What goes on at the meetings?"

"That I can't tell you. We've all been sworn to secrecy."

"I wish you would," Remo said, twisting Bobby Jay's ear until the singer's face contorted in pain.

"Oh. Oh," he moaned. "More. Oh, it hurts so good."

Remo stopped. It was no use. He was probably on the wrong track, anyway. Admiral Ives hadn't even been a member of the queen's *in* group of BPs. He was back to square one.

"Forget it," he said.

"Never," Bobby Jay sighed. "You were wonderful. I've never been pinched like that before. How are you at biting?"

"Let's get back to the admiral," Remo said disgustedly.

"Why are you so interested in him?" Bobby pouted. "He's a nobody."

"He's dead."

"See? He's so much of a nobody that I never even

heard he died. Did Rona Barrett cover it? Did he make 'Entertainment Tonight'?''

"Do you know anyone who was friends with him?"

"Certainly not. I don't associate with nobodies."

"Who'd he talk to at the party?"

"Who cares? Other nobodies. Oh, yes." He smiled up at Remo. "I know who you can talk to. Seymour Burdich."

"Who's Seymour Burdich?"

"A nobody. He runs an information service on celebrities. Finds out our favorite colors, the names of our pets, things like that. Then he publishes this drivel in some rag and sells it to fans. It keeps the riffraff out of our hair. Seymour gets to come to all the in parties. We stars like him. He's like our little mascot."

"Won't he be at Shangri-la, too?"

Bobby Jay laughed. "Oh, Seymour would never get into Shangri-la. He doesn't have a nickel."

"I thought you all liked him."

"Friendship only goes so far. One does have one's reputation to consider."

Remo looked back at the list. Burdich's name was near the bottom. His address was listed as Houston Street in the Tribeca section of New York. "Is this where Burdich lives, or where he works?" Remo asked.

"Both. You won't have any trouble finding him. One can always spot poor people in a crowd. Uh, speaking of which, you aren't *really* poor, are you?" he asked, moving away from Remo. "I mean, I *have* been talking with you for some time. I'd hate for anything to rub off."

The doorbell rang. "Consider it just another social disease," Remo said, opening the door to let himself out.

A beefy young blond boy hulked in. Bobby sighed and broke into song. "Lovely to look at, delightful to see . . ."

"I'm the ethcort," the boy said.

Chapter Five

A gray-haired man sat at a battered roll-top desk in a storefront in a section of town that looked as if it had been founded by derelicts. There was no trace of former grandeur about the bleak, trash-filled street that howled in abandonment in the dry winter wind. A sheet of newspaper blew onto the wide window of the storefront, on which the words "Stardust, Inc." were hand-lettered with white paint. The newspaper stuck in a crack in the pane, rustling shrilly.

Remo went inside. The place was clanking and churning with the din of a printing press. The solitary figure in the room bent over the desk, his long hair shaggy along the collar of his black turtleneck sweater.

"You Burdich?" Remo shouted.

"Yeah. Who do you want?" He gestured hurriedly toward several stacks of papers on the desk. They were labeled with the names of celebrities and divided by category into film, music, sports, politics, and others. "A dollar apiece. Or you can have the *Celebrity Scoop*, that's the newspaper, for a buck-fifty." He inclined his head toward the clanking printing press. "Be ready in a few seconds."

The press was spewing out pages of newsprint with headlines like "WHAT THE STARS HAVE FOR BREAKFAST" and "HOW TO MEET A ROLLING STONE." As Burdich spoke, the rumble of the press subsided and ground to a halt. Quiet filled the storefront.

"I want to talk to you about the party at the Spanglers' in Virginia last night," Remo said.

Burdich smiled expansively. His breath formed clouds in the unheated room. "Ah, yes. My other life," he said with some dignity. He twirled the ankh around his neck. "You're from a magazine, I presume."

"Yes," Remo lied.

"Which one? *Teen Idol? Rock Beat?*"

"*Stars and Stripes,*" Remo said. "I've come to ask you about Admiral Thornton Ives. The Secretary of the Navy. I understand you were talking with him last night."

"Well, I do circulate with all the guests, even if they're outsiders," he said smugly. "It's my work. Naturally, I'd rather spend my time with people of my own caliber. Military types don't make it with the group. Ives was just invited because of the senator."

"That's the second time I've heard 'the group' mentioned. Bobby Jay was talking about it, too."

Burdich raised an eyebrow. "Bobby Jay? I'm surprised he's still in town. The group travels once a month, you know."

"You know about that?"

"Oh, all about it." He puffed up with pride. "They let me in on everything they do. They confide in me. They even send me plane tickets to attend their parties." He leaned close to Remo and whispered confidentially, "You know, the BPs really are beautiful. The bigger they are, the bigger they are, I always say."

"Very profound. About the admiral—"

"Oh, he didn't count. Say, have you heard about my files?" He gestured to a bank of battered cabinets. "They're legendary. I know everything there is to know about celebs. I've even got Greta Garbo's private phone number, although that's not for sale. They trust me, you know." He winked.

"Bobby Jay called you a mascot."

Burdich rose, sputtering. "That pompous fag . . ." He gained control of himself and sat back down, smoothing the wrinkles in his tattered sweater. "I mean, Bobby's a real card. We always banter with each other. It's the group's way. A laugh a minute." He forced a half-hearted laugh.

"How do you know Bobby Jay?" Remo asked.

"Oh, I've known him forever. We went to school together, in fact. I'm tight with all of them. They love me."

"You two are the same age?" Remo asked, amazed. Burdich looked twenty years older.

"I'm fifty-two," Burdich said huffily. "Bobby Jay is three years older than I am."

Remo stared at him. It was happening again. First there was Cecilia Spangler, who looked twice as old as her own mother. And now Burdich, two years younger than a man who could have passed for his son.

"You don't believe me," Burdich sighed. "I can tell. Well, that's their game. Victims of the disease of vanity, all of them." His face hardened with bitterness. "Always running around, acting like kids. Kids! Who needs that? Who needs to look half their age, anyway? It's the fault of advertising. The Pepsi Generation has taken over."

"Uh, yuh," Remo said, bewildered by the sudden change in Burdich. "About the admiral—"

"Shangri-la," Burdich whispered, his voice breaking. "Shangri-la is only for the in group. They left me behind. It's too late. Too late."

Remo squirmed uncomfortably. He had wanted to find out about the Secretary of the Navy. And all he was getting was a string of personal obsessions about some health farm called Shangri-la.

"Too late for what?"

"Look at me!" Burdich shouted "I'm old!" He walked over to a small mirror hanging on the wall and smashed it to the floor. "Old! And I'll never be young again. They've all left me behind. Them and their money and their witch doctor. The in group. I wish I were dead. Do you hear me? Dead!" He was standing in the middle of the room, his shoulders heaving, rage burning in his eyes.

"Try deep breathing," Remo suggested.

"Oh, what's the point?" Burdich said, sweeping a stack of leaflets to the floor. "I know what I am. A hanger-on. You think I'm a hanger-on, don't you?"

"I think you're a nut," Remo said. He went on doggedly. "I'm supposed to find out about Admiral Ives, if you don't mind. He was murdered last night, and I want to find out who did it. Can you think of anyone at the party who would want to do him in?"

"He didn't count, I tell you. Nobody there cared about him. They don't care about anything except themselves. Their precious youth. Their exalted Doctor Foxx."

Remo perked up. "Foxx? Who's that?"

"The diet doctor. Felix Foxx. He's the one who started that place out there, giving the group yet another place where they may commune with their rarified peers, away from the rabble. He keeps them young. That's what separates the group from the rest of us poor suckers.''

"What do you mean, he keeps them young?"

"You heard me. He keeps them young. There's not a one of them up there in Foxx's mountain paradise that'll ever see fifty again. It's magic, I tell you. The magic of the rich. Shangri-la. The magical kingdom, where one never grows old, just like in the story. That's what he's done.'' Burdich kicked at the papers on the floor. "For those who can afford it,'' he added. "The great line of demarcation between the haves and the have-nots. Eternal youth and beauty belong only to the haves. People like you and I will show our station in life by growing old and ugly. We will wither like the leaves of winter, stricken with the infirmities of age until we die. But not *them*. Not the in group with their money and connections and their Doctor Foxx in Shangri-la. They'll never grow old. Never. They'll leave us all behind.''

Burdich's depression settled into the room like a cloud.

"Know any of the names on this list?" Remo asked with feigned cheerfulness, pulling out Cecilia's guest list.

"All of them. That's the in group. Those swine."

"You mean they're all out of town?" Remo groaned.

"Every last stinking rich one of them. It's time for the monthly meeting at Shangri-la."

Again things were brought back to Shangri-la. It seemed that no matter which direction Remo tried to lead the conversation, all roads led to the health resort in Pennsylvania.

Remo looked over at Burdich's file cabinets. "Say, do you have anything on that place?"

Burdich grunted. "Everything. I told you, I know everything about them. How they live, how they spend their money, what they do. . . .That's what makes it so hard to be on the outside."

"Can I take a look at your material on Shangri-la?"

"Never. That's in the file with Greta's phone number. I could never release that to an ordinary being."

"From the looks of you, you're an ordinary being, too."

Burdich rose. "I don't have to take that from you."

"How about taking this?" Remo said, offering up a roll of bills. Smitty kept him in currency. Not that Remo needed much, but the money came in handy at times.

"How much is there?" Burdich asked, his eyes glistening.

"Count it. Enough to get into Shangri-la, if that's what you want. Just let me see what you've got on the place."

"But I have to be worth a half-million dollars a year to join," Burdich whined.

"Say you came into an inheritance. The files?"

"I guess it wouldn't hurt. An inheritance, huh? Maybe they'd buy that." He counted the money as he pulled open a rusted drawer and extracted a single file. In it was one sheet of paper, a hand-drawn map of a region in northwestern Pennsylvania. "I did it myself, based on scattered conversations, but it's quite accurate," Burdich said. "I've even been up there to verify the accuracy of it, but they wouldn't let me in." He waved the bills in front of him. "They will now, though."

"I thought it was too late for you."

"I'll dye my hair. They'll accept me. I'll have a place. I'll be one of the BPs." He fell to his knees and grasped Remo's ankles. "Thank you. Bless you," he rasped, dragging behind Remo as far as the door.

So that was that, Remo thought. He hadn't gotten anywhere going door to door. If everybody who last saw Admiral Ives was at Shangri-la, that was where he was going. And it only cost him five or six thousand dollars in paper money.

"Sure you don't want Greta's phone number?" Burdich yelled as Remo made his way down the street.

He called Smith and told him about the fruitless interviews.

"They're *all* out of town?"

"Just about. Everyone's gone to the clinic or something in Pennsylvania named Shangri-la. The last hoople I talked to says it keeps them young."

"That's what all those places claim," Smith said.

"Yeah, I know. Only this seems to work." He explained the discrepancy between the ages of the party guests and their appearances, and gave Smith Burdich's information on Doctor Foxx.

"Many people in their fifties look twenty years younger," Smith said as the Folcroft computer banks whirred into action. "It seems to be a transitional time of life. . . . Foxx, you said?"

"Felix Foxx."

The line was silent except for the noise of the computers. "That's strange," Smith said at one point, lapsing back into silence as the bleeps and whizzes in the background increased.

"It's two degrees above zero, and I'm standing in an open phone booth," Remo said. "Can you think on your own time?"

"Very strange," Smith said. "I've got Felix Foxx here on the screen, but it's a very sketchy biography, mostly from IRS files. There seems to be no date of birth.''

''I suppose that means he doesn't exist,'' Remo said.

''It could,'' Smith answered. Harold W. Smith had total faith in his computers. They did not, as far as he was concerned, produce incorrect responses.

''He's on TV, for crying out loud,'' Remo protested. ''He's on the cover of *People* magazine.''

''And his life seems to have begun with the publication of his books,'' Smith said. ''That's when his IRS records begin. Before then, there are no bank accounts in his name, no credit cards, nothing. He seems to have materialized a year ago.''

Remo sighed. ''I'm just calling in, the way you wanted me to do. I don't care if the guy exists or not. But if you want me, I'll be at Shangri-la.'' He gave him the coordinates of the place.

''Fine. I'll check some cross-references here.''

''And one more thing. I'll need some money.''

The bitter voice at the other end rankled. ''I just gave you several thousand dollars.''

''I gave most of it to a guy for a beauty treatment.''

A low whinnying sound issued briefly from the telephone before the line went dead.

Chapter Six

Patrolman Gary MacArdle opened his desk drawer at the precinct for the twentieth time since he had come in that day and clutched the small rubber stamp hidden there.

It would be his way out. Out from under Mastercharge, the rent, the grocery bills. Out from under the colossal weight of Christmas in New York and the drain that put on his already straining bank account. The stamp, if he used it often enough, would pull him out long enough to wait for a promotion and a decent salary. The stamp would bring deliverance.

He didn't think it was illegal. Lots of the guys—even the young ones, the rookies like himself—were already taking bribes from the street dealers they were supposed to be arresting and accepting payoffs from whorehouses. But MacArdle had played it straight. He wanted to be a cop, a good cop. Still, he could see how a good cop could get twisted after his son's first Christmas, when the accounting came due in January. So MacArdle was working overtime every night, and he hardly ever saw his wife and kid anymore, and he was dead on his feet, and it didn't matter anymore if it was illegal or not—not at this point.

But Herb downstairs said it wasn't. He'd sworn to it, right there in Records. All MacArdle had to do was to stamp any report with the word *fox* in it, and he'd get a $20 cashier's check from the government. No department, no name, no tax. Just money. And Herb would get a check, too, just for adding an extra 9 at the front end of the code when he submitted the report for processing into the computer.

Checking to see that no one was looking, MacArdle pressed the stamp onto his ink pad and stamped a piece of scrap paper in the desk drawer. It printed a series of numbers beginning with three zeros.

How could it be illegal? Nobody except Herb was even going to see the report before it was processed, and Herb was in on it. And afterward, when it had gone through the computer and come out tagged and ready for filing, nobody would see it, either, unless it was a big case, but even then it would only be spotted by some computer nerd.

"But who's giving you the money?" MacArdle had asked Herb down in Records that day. Herb had done this sort of thing before. Not with *fox,* but with other key words. From time to time over the years, Herb, who'd made a career out of the 37th precinct's records, would receive a telephone call. At first he thought the lemony-sounding voice was some kind of crank, but since he had nothing to lose, he'd added the 9 to the appropriate documents just to see what would happen. What had happened was that he'd gotten a check for each report he'd put through the computer with a 9 on it. No strings. No questions. Just money.

"I don't know," Herb answered. "But it ain't the Mafia sending me U.S. government checks. My guess is the CIA."

"What? You've got to be crazy. What's the CIA want with foxes?"

"Who knows?" Herb said. "Maybe there's foxes with rabies in New York, and the CIA wants to catch them on the Q.T. All I know is they're in a hurry this time and can't wait for the reports to come down to Records through the usual channels. That's why you got to stamp every one that says 'fox' and bring it down here yourself. Got it?"

MacArdle was skeptical. "I still don't see why the CIA's so interested in this precinct."

"Don't kid yourself, kid," Herb said. "I got a friend uptown who's got a stamp just like this one. We make them up ourselves, just like the way the guy on the phone says, and when the first check comes, there's even extra to take care of the cost of the stamp. If that ain't government regulation, I don't know what is."

And so Gary MacArdle had taken the stamp and carried it with him on his beat and stayed on for overtime and had eaten supper at his desk, just in case any "fox" reports turned up, and now he slammed the desk drawer shut with a bang because any fool knew there weren't any foxes in Manhattan.

And then Doris Dumbroski came in.

She was a frowzy redhead with enough pancake on her face to turn the Hudson River orange, and she was screaming at the desk sergeant.

"What kind of a dump is this joint? What are all you bums doing around here instead of fighting crime out on the street where you belong?"

"Take it easy," the desk sergeant replied wearily. He'd been on overtime all week, too. "What's the problem?"

The redhead banged her fist on the desk. "The problem is that my roommate's been missing for ten days, and you yo-yos are hanging around here like you're waiting for a beer.''

''Have you filed a missing persons report?'' the sergeant asked.

''Yes, I filed a missing persons report,'' she mimicked. ''Last week. One day after Irma disappeared. You don't even remember. How can taxpayers be expected to—''

''We get a lot of missing persons in New York City, ma'am,'' the sergeant said. He picked up a pencil and began to write. ''Name?''

''Whose?''

''Yours.''

''Doris Dumbroski.''

The sergeant looked up from the paper. ''Oh, yeah, I remember. The stripper.''

''Watch it. I'm an exotic dancer.'' She pouffed her hair elaborately.

''Right,'' the sergeant said. ''At the Pink Pussycat. Who's your friend? The one that's missing.''

''Her name's Irma Schwartz, same as it was last week,'' Doris said.

''Okay, just a second.'' He leafed through a stack of papers on his desk. ''Schwartz, Schwartz . . .''

''What's in those?'' Doris asked.

''Homicides. Schwartz . . . Irma.'' The sergeant looked up from the paper. ''Sorry, lady,'' he said. ''Her name's down here.''

Doris stared at him, her mouth sprung open. ''A *homicide*? Like in . . . she was murdered?''

''Looks that way, lady. Sorry. She had I.D. on her, but she hasn't been identified personally yet. Just came in this afternoon. Somebody from the morgue should have called you.''

''I ain't been home,'' Doris said numbly. ''I didn't

think she'd be *murdered*, for pete's sake. Just maybe tied up with a fink."

"I guess she was," the sergeant said.

Doris Dumbroski's eyes welled up. "Okay, so what do I do now?" she choked.

The desk sergeant was solicitous. He'd seen a lot of this. "Well, if you don't mind, I'd like you to go down to the morgue with one of the police officers. If the deceased is your roommate, the officer'll fill out a homicide report. That okay with you?"

"Sure," she said lamely. "Only I can't believe Irma's dead. I mean, like she was so full of life, you know?"

"They all are," the sergeant said. "Hey, one of you guys want to take the lady to the morgue for an I.D.?"

There were no volunteers. Just about everybody on the floor was on overtime, and nobody felt like hanging around in the morgue for a grief-stricken identification and then filling out an interminable report that would drag on into the next shift.

"I mean, it was her lucky day," Doris went on.

"Depends on how you look at things, I guess," the sergeant said.

"I mean, there we was at the TV studio, and then all of a sudden Irma and Dr. Foxx were making eyes at each other, and then she was riding off in his limousine and everything. . . ."

Patrolman MacArdle dropped the rubber stamp he was toying with. "Fox?" he shouted, jumping up. "What about a fox?"

"Dr. Foxx, with two *x*'s. The diet doctor. That's who Irma went off with."

"When?"

"Monday. The last time I saw her."

The desk sergeant wrote down the name.

"I'd like to take care of this, sir," MacArdle said.

"Gonna have to take her down to the morgue, fill out the report," the sergeant said. "Your shift's almost up. Sure you want this?"

"I'm sure, sir. His name was Foxx, wasn't it?" he asked Doris.

"With two x's. He had such cute buns and everything. I mean, like, there was this chemistry between them. . . ."

"Patrolman MacArdle will take everything down," the sergeant said.

"Yes, sir," MacArdle said. The stamp was in his pocket. "Come with me, ma'am."

Doris Dumbroski sniffed and dabbed at the black smears around her eyes. "At least Irma wasn't in pain when she went," she said.

"That's good," MacArdle said sympathetically. "Wait a second. How do you know that?"

Doris sniffed. "Because she was never in pain. She was just one of those people. She never felt pain. Whoever killed her didn't hurt her. Poor Irma."

MacArdle led her out. Every last word Doris Dumbroski said was going to go into that report. It would be the fattest, fullest, best-typed report the CIA or the Mafia or whoever was handing out those checks had ever received. Happy days were here again.

Chapter Seven

The triple-zero mode was operating. Smith sat back at his console, while the Folcroft computers quietly sifted through the accumulated reports mentioning the name Foxx, from 257 police precincts around the country.

The computer had arranged the material according to Smith's programming and took out most of the dross automatically: The foxes, Phochses, and one-*x* Foxes were eliminated with whirring efficiency. The rest—the Foxxes ticketed for traffic violations, arrested for juvenile crimes, or reported as accident fatalities—had to be scrupulously, tediously scrutinized by Smith himself. He sat stone still at the console, afraid to blink, while he scanned the screen for each entry, pressing the "discard" button for every Foxx with nothing to offer.

His eyes burned. He took off his glasses for a moment and rubbed his face with a handkerchief. Then he opened them and scanned the entry on the screen. He pressed "Hold" and read the entry again.

"FOXX, FELIX, M.D. LAST SEEN WITH HOMICIDE VICTIM SCHWARTZ, IRMA L."

Smith keyed in the code. "PLEASE GIVE CAUSE OF DEATH."

The computer whirred for a moment, then flashed its version of Irma Schwartz's demise onto the screen. "SCHWARTZ, IRMA L. DEATH CAUSED BY ADMINISTRATION OF HCN THROUGH NASAL CANAL."

"EXPAND."

"HCN = HYDROCYANIC ACID, I.E. PRUSSIC ACID. LIQUID OR GASEOUS STATES. UNSTABLE. MOLECULAR CONFIGURATION. . ."

"HOLD." The computer would expand the subject forever until every scrap of available information on it was exhausted, if he let it. Smith keyed out the "Expand" function. The screen reverted to the details of Irma Schwartz's death, listing blood levels of known substances arranged by quantity. At the bottom of the list was PROCAINE. . .00001, followed by a footnote: "ALL LEVELS NORMAL EXCLUDING FINAL ENTRY."

"PROCAINE: EXPAND"

"PROCAINE = NOVOCAINE, GENERIC TERM. FOUND IN CACAO PLANT. FREQUENTLY REFINED INTO COCAINE. ALSO FOUND IN HIGHLY PURE FORM BUT SMALL QUANTITIES IN HUMAN ENDOCRINE SYSTEM. . . .

"RELATION TO SCHWARTZ, IRMA L."

"NEAR ABSENCE OF PROCAINE IN SUBJECT'S BLOOD AT TIME OF DEATH. . . DISCREPANCY WITH 000 REPORT. . . DISCREPANCY. . ."

"EXPAND DISCREPANCY."

The screen flashed back to the police report. "SUBJECT FELT NO PAIN PRIOR TO DEATH."

"What?" Smith said aloud. He asked the computer to explain.

"POLICE REPORT 000315219 QUOTE SUBJECT IS REPORTED TO HAVE FELT NO PAIN . . . DISCREPANCY WITH LOW PROCAINE LEVEL. . . ."

Smith was interested. He keyed in "PROCAINE" again and pressed the "Expand" button. The computer picked up where it had left off and spewed out volumes of information on procaine for the next twenty minutes. Among other things, Smith discovered that a body's procaine level controlled in some measure that body's tolerance for pain.

If Irma Schwartz's procaine content was nearly nil, then the strange footnote that she had suffered no pain didn't make sense. On top of it all, Felix Foxx had been with her on the day she died. It still didn't shed any light on Admiral Ives's murder, unless. . .

"UNUSUAL PROCAINE LEVELS IN AUTOPSY REPORTS FOR WATSON, HOMER G., AND IVES, THORNTON?" Smith asked.

"PROCAINE LEVELS NORMAL," the computer answered.

No connection.

Smith readjusted the program back to its former position.

The computer expanded into historical references to the drug, including various published accounts. Smith dutifully read each entry as it appeared on the screen, sifting through decades of data, working backward. In 1979 there were 165 entries on procaine, comprising the whole of the printed word worldwide, including tabloids from Sri Lanka and encyclopedias. At this rate, Smith realized, it was going to take forever.

"AMERICAN PERIODICALS ONLY," *he* keyed in. "WORD COUNT ONLY."

There were twelve mentions of the word *procaine* in

1978, all in one issue of the *Journal of American Dentistry*. Foxx's name was not mentioned. Nor was it mentioned through the entire decade of the sixties. Or the fifties. Or the forties. Smith blinked back a blinding headache.

In 1938, American newspapers and magazines printed the word *procaine* more than 51,000 times.

"HOLD. EXPAND."

The articles appeared one after the other on the screen. All of them concerned a drug scandal involving a now defunct research facility in Enwood, Pennsylvania, from which a staggering quantity of endocrinal procaine, extracted from human cadavers, was found missing. The research was being conducted, as later reports revealed, as a military experiment to increase the pain tolerances of combat soldiers.

A public outcry against scientists' fiddling around with pain experiments on Our Boys in Uniform far overshadowed any objection to the theft of the drug. As a result, the Pennsylvania facility was abandoned, the experiments aborted, and the project's head researcher quietly expatriated. His name was Vaux.

Felix Vaux.

"Vaux," Smith said, reprogramming the computer with new energy.

"EXPAND VAUX, FELIX. HEAD RESEARCHER AT ENWOOD, PA. FACILITY 416, CA. 1938," he keyed.

"VAUX, FELIX. B. AUG. 10, 1888. . . B.S. UNIVERSITY OF CHICAGO. . ."

"HOLD."

1888? That would make him ninety-four years old.

It was the wrong man. Six hours at the most powerful, omnipotent computer complex in the world, and he'd ended up with the wrong man.

Disgustedly he switched off the console. It was

going nowhere. Undoubtedly, Remo had the wrong man, too. If Smith were an ordinary computer analyst working with ordinary computers, he would have put on his twenty-year-old tweed coat at that point, and his thirty-year-old brown felt hat, and locked the catches on the attaché case containing his emergency telephone, and left for the night.

But Harold W. Smith was not ordinary. He was precise. Precise to the point where, if his peas were not positioned exactly at 9 o'clock on his plate, he would suffer with indigestion throughout the meal. So precise that he trusted almost nothing—not words, not people, not clocks. Nothing except the four items on earth that Smith considered to be adequately accurate to deserve his trust: the Folcroft computers.

And the four Folcroft computers had said, *categori ally,* that Felix Foxx, M.D., was somehow living without a date of birth. Given that much as a premise, anything else was possible.

With fresh determination he switched on the console.

"COORDINATES, ENWOOD, PA. RESEARCH FACILITY, CA. 1938?" he asked. The coordinates came up on the screen. They matched exactly those Remo had given him for Shangri La.

"Hmmm," he said. A coincidence, perhaps.

"PROBABILITY VAUX, FELIX = FOXX, FELIX?" he queried next.

"PROBABILITY FOXX = VAUX 53%, came the answer from the four things Harold W. Smith trusted alone among all beings on earth.

A better than even chance! The computers had considered the ridiculous proposition that Dr. Felix Foxx, best-selling author and eminent authority on fitness and diet, TV personality and general celebrity whose youthful face was known to millions, could be a ninety-four-year-old man named Vaux who had left the country fifty years ago in disgrace after a nationwide drug scandal, and the computers had said *fifty-three percent!*

It was the equivalent of a surgeon checking out the remains of a man burned beyond recognition, his hands and feet curled into little charred balls, his teeth no more than melted stubs sticking out of crisp-fried lips, and saying, "The odds are better than even that he'll be back on the job in a couple of weeks."

Smith was ecstatic. For no surgeon on earth could match the predictability, the surety, the breathtaking precision of the Folcroft computers. If they said fifty-three percent, then procaine could be the whole key. And Foxx the holder of that key. And Remo was on his way to someplace called Shangri-la to talk to Foxx.

"THANK YOU," he keyed in, as he always did when his work with the sublime four creatures had come to an end.

"YOU'RE WELCOME," they responded as they always did.

The precision!

Of course, there was another possibility, one unknown even to the computers, which were unique in all the universe, infallible in all properly programmed matters. The possibility that they were wrong.

Harold Smith's brow creased into a deep furrow. He felt his breath come quickly and shallowly and his heartbeat step up. Dots of perspiration formed on his brow.

Wrong? The Folcroft Four?

And then he took a deep breath, as Remo had once shown him would alleviate momentary stress, and he picked up the phone to begin the long routing connections that would lead eventually to Remo.

There was no point in considering whether or not the Folcroft computers were wrong. If they were wrong, then, as Harold Smith saw it, there would be no reason for living. The world would be thrust back into an abyss of guesswork, hypotheses, hunches, suggestions, half-truths, loopholes, double entendres, wishes, hopes, spells, incantations, and instincts. A world where being on time could mean anything within the boundaries of a geological age; where peas were not only not presented at 9 o'clock, but scattered at random all over the plate, spilling haphazardly into the mashed potatoes and canned gravy.

He shuddered.

When Smith was a young boy growing up in Vermont, his mother had introduced him, one winter day, to the feasibility of the impossible. She had taken young Harold through this quantum leap of learning with one sentence. What she said was, "It's not snowing today because it's too cold to snow."

Too cold to snow? Was she kidding? What could be colder than snow? It was practically ice, only fluffy. When it gets cold, it snows. Any colder than that, and . . .

It would be too cold to snow.

The concept had intrigued the precise young Harold W. Smith beyond description. Later, he would come to group the thought of unsnowable cold with other such mystifying paradoxes as liquid oxygen and dry ice. How do you breathe a liquid? Doesn't it clog up your nose? When you put dry ice in a glass of water, does it suck it all up like a sponge?

Even after he understood the workings of these miraculous phenomena, Smith continued to remember them with vestigial traces of awe. It was part of the grand scheme of things. Some things just *were*. Dry ice was one of them, and the immutable correctness and utter truth of the Folcroft computers was another, and that was all there was to it.

No, the computers weren't wrong. There was a fifty-three percent chance that Foxx was Vaux and was consequently ninety-four years old and perhaps involved with a drug named procaine to such an extent that he was willing to murder an unknown woman for the minuscule amount in her body; and that somehow this series of possibilities would lead to the combat-type killings of two military leaders, spaced one day apart.

The phone at the Shangri-la address kept ringing.

There was a fifty-three percent chance that Remo was in the middle of something even the Folcroft computers would have called strange.

Chapter Eight

"You're *how* old?" Remo gasped, switching on the lamp with its pink light bulb.

It had been great sex. Perfect sex. Hot, inventive, passionate, tender, first-time-in-a-car sex. Only this was in a bed, and the spectacular blonde beside him had just shattered the women's record for duration and frequency. She was not only fast, she was super-sonic. And good, really good. There hadn't been any romance to sweeten the pie, as it were, either. No meaningful talks, no outpouring of private dreams. Just plain old jump-on-the-bones sex, and it had been the best he'd known since Roseanne Ziewiecki let him have it in the baseball field behind the orphanage when he was fourteen.

Roseanne knew what she was doing, but the pale blonde with the kitten face and the ocean-blue eyes had to be the most experienced sexual partner ever placed on the planet. And now Remo knew why.

"I'm seventy," she purred, stroking his thigh. "And a half."

"*Seventy*?" He had already withered beyond re-demption. That had happened the first time she told him her age. Now, with the second blast of the same bad news, his stomach churned as he was swept by a wave of oedipal guilt trimmed around the edges with a border of pure absurdity. "Seventy?"

"There's no need for pretense here," she cooed. She cradled Remo's hand expertly in her own. At seventy, Remo thought, she'd had her share of hand holding. "We're all young here. That's what we pay for." She laughed softly. "Go on, admit it. You're up there, too, aren't you?"

"No, no part of me is up there," Remo said truthfully. "Down. Very down."

She stood up in a huff, her perfect flanks glistening without a hint of a stretch mark in the moonlit bedroom. Remo tried to piece together the events that had brought him here to this bed, where a seventy-year-old woman was undulating before him with the healthy abandon of a young colt.

He and Chiun had arrived at Shangri-la less than an hour before. Getting into the place had presented no problem after he ditched the car he'd rented at the Enwood train depot. No cars were permitted on the grounds. "They detract from the timeless ambience of Shangri-la," the guide had said haughtily.

The guide—a chauffeur, as it turned out—drove the guests through the snow-covered hills, along narrow roads, and into a huge landscaped clearing in the middle of nowhere, surrounded by a high wrought-iron fence with an even higher electronically controlled gate.

"Welcome to Shangri-la," the guide said in the midst of the vast snow-capped greenery where the road stopped.

Chiun speculated unpleasantly that Shangri-la was an expensive version of KOA Kampgrounds, with the lot of them getting their massages and carrot cocktails, while building igloos for the night. But as they walked, the place, *the* Shangri-la, mecca of dreams, giver of youth, refueling station for Bobby Jay's BPs en route to the rigors of life on the Mediterranean, appeared.

It was a monstrous place, a mansion of Victorian dimensions, but with the requisite Hollywood touches of an Olympic-sized swimming pool and klieg lights calling to the illustrious guests like beacons in the dark. Still, despite the elegant trappings, there was something sinister about Shangri-la. A word out of old vampire novels kept springing into Remo's mind. *Unwholesome.* The place had an unwholesome air about it. Remo could almost smell it. Chiun said he *did* smell it.

"Or maybe it is just the smell of so many whites," he said.

The guests themselves were no longer any surprise to Remo. Many were famous names, which Remo could dimly pick out from among his early memories. All were robust, attractive, stylish, rich, and young. Senator Spangler and his wife stood by the fireplace inside the sprawling parlor of the house, chatting with a group of handsome young people dressed in their expensive best. Bobby Jay was standing by the grand piano in the corner snapping his fingers and singing an off-key version of "I Love the Boy I'm Near."

With a brief shake of his head, Remo refused a martini thrust into his field of vision. Chiun refused also, by shattering the glass in midair so quickly that the waiter's brain didn't register the old man's discontent—he continued to peddle the drink, which was no longer a drink in his fingers, but an olive.

The canapés were as bad. "White man's food,"

Chiun sneered. "A chicken's liver surrounded by pig fat and set atop a lump of green cheese on a cracker. No wonder you are all slothful and mindless. Look at what you eat."

"This is just a snack," Remo explained. "Dinner hasn't been served yet."

"I see. One eats before eating so as to be prepared for eating. The labyrinthine processes of the white mind."

"We'll skip the canapés," Remo told the waiter.

And then there was the blonde. One minute she was slinking through the crowd in her red-sequined spray-on gown, demurely eyeballing Remo, and the next minute they were upstairs in bed together, with the blonde purring and stroking and doing the knock-your-socks-off thing that she did. And Remo forgot all about the 52 idiot steps to a woman's ecstasy, since this one was ecstatic enough for an army, during the first bout of hand holding.

And then she dropped the bomb about being seventy freaking years old.

"What'd you have to say that for?" Remo asked miserably, sure in his secret heart that he would never enjoy himself in bed again.

"Quit acting so naïve," she said. Then she stopped and looked at him with something like amusement. "Or is this your first time?"

"First time for what?"

"Let me see your arms."

"What?" He struggled, but she was on him again, and was holding the inside of his left arm up to the pink bedside lamp. "Not a mark," she said, apparently amazed. "Why, you're a virgin."

"To what?"

"The *injections*," she said. "Dr. Foxx's injections."

She took his hands in hers. "I don't want to scare you or anything, but I hope you know what you're getting into here."

"I don't know what you're talking about," Remo said. "I don't know anything that's going on in this screwball place."

She held out her own arms. "This, for one thing." Beneath the pink spill of light, the inside of her arms looked like antique wood, tracked with so many holes you could sift flour through them.

"I know, the tracks are ugly, I have plastic surgery done to cover the marks every five years. But that's the least of it." Her voice was soft and faraway.

"Jesus," Remo said, aghast. "How long have you been shooting up that happy juice?"

"A long time," she said, looking levelly at Remo. "An awfully long time. I told you, I'm seventy years old. I've had the injections for most of those seventy years."

"Oh, knock it off," Remo said. "Whatever those marks mean, they don't mean you're an old lady."

"But I am. We're all old here."

"Look. Bobby Jay might look younger than fifty-five. Mrs. Spangler could pass for less than the fifty-eight her daughter claims. But if you're seventy, I'm Methuselah. Now, why are you handing me a line like that?"

"It's no line," she said. "What's your name?"

"Remo."

"I'm Posie Ponselle." Remo started. "You've heard of me?"

"I've heard the name," Remo said. "Some movie star in the thirties or something."

"They compared me with Garbo," she said wistfully. "The Love Goddess."

Remo looked at her askance. "Lady, if you expect me to believe that you're Posie Ponselle—"

"You don't have to believe anything. I just want you to know what you're walking into if you take that first injection tomorrow."

"Okay," he sighed. She, not Remo, had broken the spell. But it was just as well, he thought. It was time to get back to business. "When did you meet Foxx?"

"Forty years ago," Posie said without a blink.

"Come *on*."

"You asked."

"All right," Remo waffled. If he had to listen to another crock from another nutcase before he could get a scrap of information, well, that was how it went in this assignment. There wasn't a sane person in the place. "Go ahead."

"It was in Geneva. You see, just before the war broke out, my movies weren't doing too well. I was getting too old, they said. I was twenty-eight." She took a cigarette from her beaded bag and lit it. "So I went to Switzerland for a series of age-retardant treatments at a new clinic I'd heard about. Foxx was there."

"The same Foxx?"

She nodded. "He never ages. And his patients don't either, as long as they keep up the treatments. But if they can't. . ." Her voice trailed off to a mumble.

"If they can't, what?"

She exhaled and ground out the fresh cigarette with trembling fingers. "Never mind. But you have to keep them up. You have to get the injections every day. That's what I want you to understand before you accept the first treatment."

"I thought you folks came here once a month," Remo said.

"For a new supply. Foxx gives us exactly thirty days' worth of the formula. Every thirty days we have to show up with cash—no checks, no credit—or else he stops the treatments on the spot."

Her voice quavered. Dizzy dame, Remo thought. Most women, he supposed, worried about their looks. But this one acted like getting to be thirty days older was the end of the world.

"Okay," he said. "But the thing I can't understand is why Foxx keeps this place such a secret. If he really does have some kind of magic formula for keeping people young forever, he could make a fortune."

"He does," Posie said. "But not from us. The income from the thirty guests at Shangri-la would barely pay for the upkeep of the place."

"What else has he got going?"

"I don't know exactly. Not now, anyway. But some funny things were going on years ago, when I worked for him."

"When was that?"

"In the forties and fifties. I ran out of money for the treatments after a few years in Switzerland. I tried to get my agent in Hollywood to find me another picture, but nobody in the business wanted to take a chance on me. Commercial flights to Europe were practically nonexistent during the war, so I couldn't get back to talk to them myself. Besides, I didn't have enough cash to take a supply of the formula with me back to America. So I stayed."

"What kind of job did Foxx offer you?"

"The usual," she said. "At first I was his mistress. He was rough, really bad. He liked to hurt. I hated him, but I needed the injections. In time, though, he got tired of me. I was glad about that. But he'd grown to trust me. By the time he was ready to move his operation here to Shangri-la, I was keeping some of his books.''

''Oh?'' Remo said, interested. ''What was in them?''

''Different things. The income from the Geneva clinic, mostly. That's where he produced the formula. In those days, he was gone quite a bit, and I'd run the clinic for him. There weren't any guests there by then, of course. Foxx wanted to get back to America, so he had cut all his patients off. . . .''

She started to tremble. ''What's wrong?'' Remo asked.

''Nothing. I was just remembering. . . .'' She shrugged it off. ''Anyway, sometimes he'd leave for months at a stretch. During those times, while I was at the clinic in Switzerland, he'd give me instructions over the phone. Sometimes he wanted me to pick up these packages that were left in weird places— alleys, old warehouses, places like that. They were always wrapped in brown paper, those packages.''

''What was in them?''

She looked up. ''Gold,'' she said softly. ''That's what was strange. Millions came in that way. Always brown packages dropped somewhere with bricks of gold inside.''

''Did you know who left them?''

''How could I? They were just dumped. But that's not all of it. Something else began happening around that time, too. Foxx started calling and telling me to ship out huge quanties of the formula to the States.''

''Here?''

"No. It was odd. He wanted me to send them all to South Dakota."

"South Dakota?"

"Don't ask me why South Dakota. The post office boxes where I was supposed to send them were all over the Black Hills region."

"Is this still going on?"

"I don't know. The clinic in Geneva was sold. He keeps the supplies for the guests in the basement here, but I don't know where he produces the formula these days. I don't work for him any more."

She spoke as if she were in a daze. "He was going to cut me off when he left Switzerland. He said that if I couldn't pay for the drug in one way or another, I could do without it."

"It might have been the kindest thing he ever did for you," Remo said.

She smiled ruefully. "Maybe. In a way, it might have been. I married a Swiss industrialist I'd met while Foxx was on one of his long visits to America. Fortunately, he was quite wealthy. Before Foxx left Geneva for good, he sold us a quantity of the formula, enough for several months. My husband wanted to try it, so I began giving him the injections, too."

"Just two happy little addicts," Remo said.

She started to shake again. "I *introduced* him to it," she whispered. "He was killed in an automobile accident two months later. I saw him after he died. . . ." A low moan issued from her throat. She looked as if she were on the verge of screaming.

"Posie? Posie!" He shook her back into the present.

"Remo," she said. "Oh, please don't take the treatment. I know what it does, even after one time. I've seen it. Don't. . .don't. . . ."

She was sobbing. "Hey, take it easy," Remo said, rocking her in his arms.

"Get out of here as soon as you can. Before it's too late for you, too."

He kissed her. And suddenly he didn't care how old she was. There was something about Posie Ponselle that made him feel like the happiest man who ever lived, something womanly and yet almost unbearably fragile, as if at any moment she would disintegrate in his arms.

They made love again. It was even better than the last time, because there was more of Posie in it—not just Posie, the beautiful blonde who knew every imaginable way to please a man, but another, wise, sad, infinitely tender.

"If you don't watch out, I'm going to fall in love with you," Remo said.

Her smile faded. "Don't do that," she said. "For your sake, don't. Just leave."

"I can't. Not until I've talked to Foxx."

"What for?" she said, alarmed. "You're not a spy for him or anything, are you?"

Remo shook his head. "Posie, I can't tell you what I am just now, but I think Dr. Foxx is more dangerous than you know. I've got to see him personally."

She looked at him for a long moment. "If I arrange a meeting, will you promise to leave? Without taking the treatment?"

"I won't take the treatment," Remo said.

"Fair enough." She put on her dress and kissed him good-bye.

She closed the door behind her. Remo sat in silence in the pool of pink light cast by the bedside lamp.

Her *arms*! If half of Posie's strange story was true he would have to get her out of here. Felix Foxx was into a lot more than the health resort business.

He felt a strange vibration behind the bed. He searched for the source, but saw nothing except a loose telephone wire that obviously had been cut deliberately. He held it up. The buzz vibrated through his fingers.

That was funny. There wasn't any ringing in the rest of Shangri-la, so every other phone in the house must have been disconnected, too. He manipulated the wires into the telephone. By the fifteenth soundless ring, he made the connection.

"Who is it?" he said into the mouthpiece.

"Smith," came the lemony voice. "I'm using the phone in my briefcase. If there's no one with you, we should be able to talk privately."

"Oh, it's private, all right. The telephone lines have all been cut. How'd you get the number?"

"The computers, of course."

"Of course," Remo said. He told Smith about the daily injections and everything he could remember about Posie Ponselle except for her sterling performance between the sheets. "She says that she's seventy years old, and that Foxx is even older than she is."

"Oh. Oh. Oh." Smith sounded as if he were about to fall off a tall building.

"What is it?"

"Quiet, please." The phone crackled with the whirr and hum of the Folcroft Four in action. "Good God," Smith uttered, his voice shaky. "Seventy-eight percent."

"Seventy-eight percent of what?"

Smith told him about the Foxx/Vaux theory and about the scandal involving procaine in 1938. "There's a seventy-eight percent chance that this Dr. Foxx is the same Vaux who was working on the procaine experiments fifty years ago. Foxx may have killed a woman for the procaine in her body. An Irma Schwartz, if that's any help."

"How about Ives? And the Air Force guy?"

"Their procaine levels are normal. There's still no connection."

"Any word from the military?"

"Nothing," Smith said. "If you're running after the wrong man, then whoever killed them will be running around loose forever. What have you picked up from the other guests—besides this woman? Frankly, Remo, that story about the gold drop-offs and the formula shipments to South Dakota doesn't make sense. Those facts don't even compute."

"I think she was telling the truth," Remo said.

"Until it computes, her information is inconsequential," Smith said crisply. "Who else have you spoken with?"

"Well, I'm getting to that," Remo said, pulling on his trousers. The wires in his makeshift telephone circuit were welding together. The connection was breaking fast.

"We haven't any time to waste," Smith pressed, barely audible among the crackles and static on the line.

"Okay, okay," Remo said. "I'll be here for another twenty-four hours or so, since tomorrow's the big day around here—Smitty?" He juggled the wires in the phone, but no sound came. The line was dead.

Which was just as well, since at that moment the six-foot, four-inch frame of a man wearing what looked to be a white toga came flying past the window outside.

"Wa-wa-wa," the man called as he zoomed upward toward the roof. And past the roof, toward the stars.

Remo looked to the snow-covered garden below, already sure of who would be down there.

A crowd of onlookers near the swimming pool, similarly attired and shivering in the cold, gasped and shrieked piteously as a second man, smaller and with graying hair, blasted off into space. In the center of the throng stood Chiun, his arms folded triumphantly across his chest, his face serene.

"Oh, bulldookey," Remo said. The first man, the giant, turned in an arc overhead and began his dive, nose first, like a white-sheathed warhead. He had stopped wailing, his features set rigidly in a mask of unadulterated terror, as he sped downward alongside the house. He was near enough to the walls to touch them, if he felt like skinning his palms on his way to eternity.

"Hang on!" Remo called, throwing open the window and hoisting himself up to his knees.

The man's stone face made a slow turn. "To what?" he moaned.

"To me." He stretched out his arms, slowly pivoting so that he was facing up, supported by the backs of his knees against the window frame. He was directly in line with the falling body.

A woman below screamed and fainted. "This is terrible," another said.

"Quite terrible," Chiun said sympathetically. "Remo is always interfering."

"How could you do such a thing?" a muscular beach-blanket type yelled to Chiun.

"Oh, it was nothing," he said, beaming modestly.

"Just a small upward thrust. It is an elementary maneuver. . . ."

But no one was listening. Everyone was watching the thin young man with the thick wrists trying fruitlessly to save two men falling in space, one behind the other, as they sped toward the hard frozen ground.

"No, no," said the man in the air who was about to meet his maker three seconds before his associate.

"Stretch out," Remo shouted.

"Mama!. . ."

"Stretch out!"

He curled into a fetal position. It was going to make it tougher for Remo. Tougher, but still no sweat. It was an easy job, almost embarrassingly easy. Chiun would laugh him all the way back to Folcroft if Remo couldn't manage to catch two falling people, while supported by his knees. By his toes, maybe. . . .

No, not even then. During Remo's years of training, Chiun had hurled boulders toward him off steel levers thirty feet long and expected him to stop them with a three-finger bounce, while treading water—without getting wet above the waist. *That* was difficult. This was nothing.

But when he caught the two men, snatching at their strange flowing garments with a manipulation of his fingers that spread the fabric out and cradled them inside it like stork-delivered babies, the crowd below went crazy. They acted as though he'd just come back from Mars with little red men for all of them to play with. The woman who had fainted earlier looked up to Remo with a face radiant with wonder and shouted, "Bless you!" The others gave him three cheers and babbled excitedly about what a hero Remo was.

Only Chiun saw the true insignificance of the maneuver, and he was looking at the weeping, shrieking faces around him as if he'd been tossed into a lunatic asylum. Remo shrugged as he hauled the flailing, wild-eyed men into the house through the window.

"Thank you, thank you," the gray-haired man burbled, falling to his knees and kissing Remo's still bare feet.

"Hey, watch it," Remo said irritably. It was bad enough that he'd had to perform grade-school tricks in front of a bunch of spectators, but having some nut smear his lips all over Remo's toes was pushing the limit.

The man raised his tear-stained face. "It's fate," he intoned.

It was Seymour Burdich, finally divested of his black turtleneck and ankh and draped in the Grecian gown that seemed to be the fashion at Shangri-la.

"You again," Remo said.

"You've given me my life. You're a true hero. I'll do anything for you. Anything?"

Remo thought. "Anything?"

"Anything."

"Good. Wait till Jumbo here comes around, and I'll tell you what you can do for me."

Burdich scuttled toward the windowsill, where the other man Remo had saved, the enormous one, was just coming to. "Mama?" the big red-haired man said weakly.

"Remo. Get your act together."

The stairway outside the bedroom was already thundering with the footfalls of the onlookers. They were coming up like an army. The big man cleared his throat and thrust his hand out at Remo.

"Son," he said, his voice now booming with control, "A young man like you can go far. I'm president of Amalgamated Steel and Iron, Houston, and I want you to know there's a vice-presidency waiting for you."

"Can it," Remo said. "Do me a favor?"

"You name it, pard."

"Anything," Burdich said. "I will walk to the ends of the earth for you. I will scale mountains. I will walk on hot coals—"

"I want you to tell everybody that you got up there by yourselves."

"What?" Burdich said, astonished.

Amalgamated Steel drawled, "Listen, boy, some old Chinaman threw me up there, and I'm going to see to it he gets his little yeller nose caved in."

Remo tried to reason with him. "How's it going to make you look if you go around telling everybody that a little old guy weighing a hundred pounds just threw you ten stories into the air?"

"But gawldurn it, they saw it with their own eyes."

"Appearances can be deceiving," Remo philosophised.

"Re-mo! Re-mo!" the crowd shouted in the hallway behind the door.

The big man thought. At last he shook his head and said, "Nope. Sorry, son. You're a fine boy, but justice must be done. Truth is truth, and justice is justice."

Remo picked him up by the ankles and thrust him out the window again. "And accidents are accidents," he said.

Amalgamated roared as he dangled upside-down, his red hair blowing in the breeze. "Okay! I did it myself." Remo pulled him back in. "Though I'll be gawldurned if anybody's going to believe that," he added. "How was I supposed to have gotten myself up there? Playing hopscotch?"

"Tell them it's an old family secret," Remo said. He turned to Burdich, who had positioned himself back at

Remo's feet and was kowtowing in a rapid series. "That okay with you?" Remo asked.

"Anything. I will swallow toads. I will prostrate myself before the hordes."

"Fine. Prostrate yourself before the horde outside the door for a while."

"Anything you say," Burdich said somberly.

"You too," Remo said, motioning for the big man to leave. "Tell them the story."

When they had left, Remo dashed back toward the window. Chiun was still standing below, looking up scornfully. "Wait for me, Little Father," he said. He slowly lowered himself out of the window, pressing his hands and feet against the surface of the wall. Then he was scaling down the brick as effortlessly as a spider, somersaulting at the last moment to a standing position on the ground.

Chiun's eyes were burning into his. "They called you a hero," the old man said sullenly.

Remo led him to a small recessed window along the house's foundation. "I want to check out the basement," he said.

"A hero! For a piece of work any chimpanzee could have performed."

"What can I do about it?" Remo said, raising the window and snaking inside. Chiun followed. "They didn't know how easy it was to catch those two guys. There's no harm done."

"No harm? No harm? Harm has been done to me. I was the one who sent those louts to the heavens in two perfect opposing spirals. Did you not see the pattern formed when the bodies began their descent?" He was jumping up and down and screeching like a mad bird.

"Quiet down," Remo whispered, distracted. Posie

Ponselle may have been telling the truth, whether what she said computed with Smitty or not. If she was, then some tangible evidence of her weird story might be in the basement. "Uh, that was good work, Chiun. Really super."

"Do not congratulate me with your cheap accolades. It was not super. It was perfect. One of the most exceptional double-spiral air blows ever executed in all the teachings of Sinanju. But do I, the Master himself, receive so much as a 'well done' from those insipid white persons?" He pointed disdainfully toward the upper floors of the mansion. "Is there even one attempt to reward me with some useless trinket?"

"Chiun," Remo whispered. Beneath the rickety stairwell were stacked dozens of sealed cartons. Each contained thirty vials of clear liquid. "Here's the stuff for the guests."

Chiun paid no attention. "Naturally, not one among them sought to praise the Master of Sinanju in his glory."

Remo felt along the cobwebbed walls of the cellar. The foundation stones had been laid more than a hundred years before. The mortar around them was cracked and mildewed. He tapped the stones rhythmically, one hand following the other, until his hands were flying and the walls vibrated with a low rumble. He followed the stones around three walls. As he approached the last wall, near a dank corner, the sound of his tapping changed almost imperceptibly. He tried the stone again. Unmistakable. There was a hollow place behind it.

Drumming his fingers along the mortar surrounding the stone, he ground it into flying dust. It was new mortar, recently laid. He removed the stone easily, and felt in the hollow behind it. A few inches from the surface was what felt like a tarpaulin covering a large geometric shape.

Chiun continued to pace around the basement, expounding on his various psychological injuries. "No," he said. "Instead they look to *you*. You who have done nothing more than hang gracelessly from a window. . . ."

"Bingo," Remo said. Beneath the tarp was a huge cube of shimmering gold. He craned to see the dimensions of the cube inside the wall. "I wonder how many millions this is worth."

"Are you listening to me?" Chiun groused.

"No." He lifted the stone back into place. Upstairs, he heard the insistent chanting coming from the hallway outside the upstairs bedroom. "Come on. I've seen what I wanted to see. We've got to get back up there."

"Why?" Chiun said, scaling up the wall after Remo. "Have you not received enough undue praise for one day?"

"I just want everything to look normal," he explained. "I still haven't talked to Foxx yet. Until I do, I want everybody to think we're just a couple of nice guys."

"I am nice," Chiun said. "I am the nicest, sweetest, most loving—"

"You practically killed two men," Remo whispered as he vaulted back into the room. "Do you know how much attention we would have drawn if they'd died?"

"Ridiculous," Chiun said. "No one would have noticed. They all look the same, dressed in those obscene things."

"I can't argue all day. The plain fact is, you assaulted two people who weren't doing anything wrong."

"Weren't—" Chiun staggered back, speechless. "But did you not see the extreme offense they were perpetrating upon my being?"

"How could I? I was in here."

Chiun's face was steely. "With that woman of the yellow hair and deformed chest, no doubt."

"That's beside the point. What'd they do?"

"They sought to shame me publicly," Chiun said, his eyes downcast. "Publicly. In the middle of a parade."

"You can do better than that," Remo said. "A parade? Out in the snow? Come on, Chiun."

"It is true. While you were up here procreating with the bulbous white thing, the rest of these fools disappeared and came back wearing those nightgowns and holding candles and chanting and marching. They marched around the room. Then they formed ranks and marched outside. As it was the first interesting thing these slugs had done all evening, I deigned to join them. For their benefit I sang to them the song of the Marching Cypriots, who were also fools in nightgowns."

"So?"

"So then I was assaulted. *I*. Not they."

"For singing?"

Chiun sighed. "No, dim one. No one assaults the Master of Sinanju for his faultless singing. It is as the song of the winged bird—"

"For what, then?" Remo asked, exasperated.

"For refusing to wear one of their nightgowns!" Chiun shrieked. "Can you understand nothing? Those two men dared to halt the parade to demand that I remove my splendid robe and replace it with primitive white garb. It was shocking."

"Look, I don't know why they're wearing those things, either," Remo said. "But it still wasn't any reason to deck them."

"I did not deck them," Chiun said with dignity. "I exercised the double-spiral air blow. Barely a touch. Oh, it was so beautiful. . . ."

"Well, it didn't happen, okay?" Remo said, listening to the rising chant of the crowd calling for him outside the door. "Those two guys you almost killed are willing to say you never touched them."

Chiun smiled. "That is kind, Remo. But even the Master of Sinanju cannot execute a spiral air blow without any touching whatsoever. Oh, it was slight, just the merest flick, but nevertheless—"

"I mean they're going to say they got up there by themselves."

Chiun's eyes flashed open into saucers. "What?"

"And then nobody'll try to throw us out. We've got to stay here long enough for me to put the screws to that Dr. Foxx."

"*Themselves?* Those two flabby hoglets? Surely you're joking."

"It's the only way, Chiun."

Chiun glared at him. "*Et tu*, Remo," he said. "To think how I have trusted you, nourished you with my sweat and my work, only to be stabbed in the back by so ungrateful a pupil as to sully the glorious House of Sinanju itself."

"Trust me," Remo said, walking toward the door.

"Trust?" Chiun said with a weak puff of a laugh. "He speaks to me of trust. He who has thrust the dagger into my breast."

"Hi, gang," Remo said to the throng outside.

Waves and cheers went up as Burdich and the Texan warded off the searching hands.

"Re-mo! Re-mo!"

"Oh, my heart," Chiun groaned.

"Speech! Speech!"

"No, really," Remo said, smiling shyly. "It was no big deal. These fellows just got themselves into a little trouble, right?" He elbowed Burdich in the ribs.

"Right."

"He has even prepared his accomplices," wailed Chiun from the interior of the bedroom.

"Hey, who's in there?" someone asked.

"Nobody," Remo said quickly.

"Nobody!" wailed Chiun.

"I've got an idea," Remo said. "Let's all go downstairs."

"Marvelous," called out the purring voice of Posie Ponselle. She snaked forward and touched the Texan's hand, which was blocking the path to Remo. "Down, boy," she said, clasping Remo's hand. "Dr. Foxx is waiting to meet our hero." She winked at him and whispered, "As promised."

"Thanks, Posie."

"Our hero," a woman nearby gushed.

A sound like a protracted case of Cheyne-Stokes breathing emanated from the room behind Remo.

Foxx sat in his study, wearing a silk Sulka dressing gown and holding a spoon of cocaine up to his nose. He greeted Remo with a powerful snort. "The man of the hour," he said, offering the spoon to Remo.

"No thanks. It gives me zits."

Foxx smiled. It was the same affable, smooth smile that had charmed the hearts of millions. "We're all grateful to you," he said. "Those two fellows would never have made it without you."

"Piece of cake," Remo said uneasily. He didn't want Foxx to have much idea of what he could do. It was always better to be underestimated. "Lucky accident."

"Mmmmm." He snorted another noseful. "Are you here for the treatments, Mr. . ."

"Remo. Just call me Remo. Yes, sir, Doc. Just one of the boys."

"I must say, you seem like rather an unlikely candidate for our clinic," Foxx said. "Most of our guests are afraid of impending middle-age. You appear to be enjoying the pink of youth."

Remo didn't like Foxx. There was something oozy about him. And the smell. . . . There *was* a smell at Shangri-la. It was stronger around Foxx than anywhere else.

"No time like the present, I always say."

"But you haven't registered."

"I'm a late arrival, I guess."

Foxx cleared his throat. "One of our guests, Bobby Jay, recognized you in your heroic stand outside the window. He claims you visited him earlier today at his apartment."

"Well, yes. . . ."

"And that you were interested in military matters."

"Not really," Remo stammered. He was being found out awfully fast. He had wanted to approach Foxx slowly, to watch his movements, to follow him until the doctor led him to something of importance.

But that was gone now. Foxx knew something was up. "I guess I was mistaken," he said.

"I want to inform you here and now that neither this

clinic nor myself have any connection to the military. Furthermore, outsiders are forbidden at Shangri-la." He scrutinized Remo with distaste. "What is your line of work, anyway?"

"Just odd jobs," Remo said. "You know, strong back, weak mind. I just heard things about this place, and I wanted to check it out."

Keep it low, Remo told himself. When the proper moment came, he would force Foxx into a position to move fast. But don't scare him now. Keep it nice and easy.

"And what have you discovered in your checking?" Foxx asked condescendingly.

"Oh, nothing much," Remo said. "Just the phones. Did you know all the lines were cut?"

"Really," Foxx said drily.

"Yeah. Think I could take a look at them? I'm pretty good with things like that. Maybe I could get them to work again."

"That won't be necessary," Foxx said. "They were cut on purpose."

"Why?" Remo asked innocently.

"Because we don't like strangers here." Foxx's tone became menacing. "They become tempted to communicate with those on the outside."

"Why'd you let me stay this long, then?"

"You were—shall we say, detained by one of our guests," Foxx said. "Rest assured, Miss Ponselle has heard about her behavior. And will hear even more."

Remo smiled. "But now the other guests don't want you to kick me out, either," he said.

Foxx sniffed haughtily. "Since you were so helpful to our two troubled guests, you and your aged friend will be granted special dispensation to remain for the Exit of Age ceremony tonight. However—"

"The Exit of Age?"

Foxx made a deprecating gesture. "A small ritual we perform on the eve of the dispensation of monthly treatments. The guests like it. You may remain for the Exit of Age, but I'm afraid you must leave before tomorrow morning. This is an expensive clinic, after all. It really wouldn't be fair to allow you to remain alongside paying guests. You understand." He was so fatherly, so firm yet gentle, so practiced in his manner.

So phony, Remo thought. But keep it low. If he wanted them out by tomorrow, the moment when he would take action was coming up soon. All it would take, then, would be a little push from Remo, and Foxx would go running like a scared rabbit. With Remo right behind him.

"Of course, I understand," Remo said in his best orphan-boy voice. "And I appreciate your letting my friend and me stay for the Exit of Age. We sure wouldn't want to miss that. No, sir." Just a little push.

"That will be all," Foxx said, dismissing Remo with a wave of his cocaine spoon.

Now, Remo thought. Push now. "Oh, by the way, Doc."

"Yes," Foxx said irritably.

"A girl I know is just crazy about you. She went out with you once."

"Really," the doctor said, uninterested.

"Yeah. She told me to tell you hello."

Foxx smiled tightly and nodded.

"She said she didn't even think you'd remember her, but I said you looked like a great guy on television. I told her, 'Irma,' I said, 'I just know he'll remember you. He looks like a great guy.' That's what I said."

Foxx stiffened noticeably.

"Irma was sick for a while, but she's all better now. I knew you'd want to hear that. Irma Schwartz. Remember her?"

"That's imposs—" Fox began, rising from his seat. He swallowed once, and the flicker of discomfort was gone from his face. "That's too bad," he said smoothly. "Do give Irma my regards."

"I knew you'd remember," Remo said, smiling. It was time to twist the screws. "I hear you remember lots of things. Like what happened here in this house back in 1938."

Foxx blanched.

"Some kind of drug experiments, weren't they, Doctor . . . *Vaux?*"

"I don't know what you're talking about," Foxx said quickly. "You must have me confused with someone else."

"Oh, I don't think so, Dr. Vaux. Because those experiments were with procaine, weren't they? And that's what you're shooting up these rich idiots with, isn't it? How many guests are here, anyway? Thirty, something like that?"

"I—I don't recall. . . ."

"Thirty people, at one pop a day apiece. That isn't that much procaine. So, no matter how much you charge them for it, it doesn't amount to that much money. And yet you've got about a million dollars in gold stashed away in your basement. Unless the publishers of your books are paying in gold bullion these days, I just don't see how you've come to acquire that."

"You're going to have to leave," Foxx said, his hands trembling visibly.

"So I say to myself, 'Remo, maybe something's going on here.' But it's just a thought."

He turned to go. At the door, he touched his fingers to his forehead in salute to the white-faced, stricken-looking man who was gripping the arms of his chair as if he were riding a roller coaster gone haywire.

The push had worked. "Thanks for your hospitality, Doctor. Maybe we'll see each other again."

The doctor didn't answer. Long after the door closed with a soft click behind Remo he remained glued to his chair, his knuckles white on the armrests.

Chapter Nine

Remo had been talking to himself for the past ten minutes. Chiun was in the room with him, the same bedroom where Remo and Posie had discovered one another, but the old man was on a different plane. He sat on the floor in full lotus, his middle fingers and thumbs pressed together as he chanted Korean mantras in a low buzz. The only response Remo could get out of him were variations in the buzz. Intense buzzes signaled disagreements with Remo's seemingly solitary arguments. Chiun, Remo knew, was not about to dignify Remo's presence with words. Being a hero had relegated him to the dungheap of Chiun's emotional backyard in the first place. And, judging from the frenzy of the buzzes, Chiun wasn't that crazy about his new proposition, either.

"It's an *assignment*, Little Father," he pleaded, holding out the white toga toward the old man, who continued to buzz serenely. "It doesn't mean anything. We'll wear them on top of our clothes."

There was a quick snort to assert Chiun's views on the idea, followed by the same low Korean buzz. The old man's eyes were closed.

"The ceremony's going to start any minute, and

Foxx is primed. He knows we're on to him, and he's scared. If he's going to do something stupid, now's the time he'll do it.''

Chiun rolled his eyes and continued to buzz.

"He'll send a message to somebody or move something, or talk to somebody in the place. I tell you, he's going to show his colors.''

Chiun's face squeezed together in fury as the buzz pitched into a shriek and broke off. "As you showed your colors?'' he burst out, unable to contain himself any longer. "As you duped those lunatics into believing you were a hero for executing a second-year exercise, while the feats of the Master of Sinanju were attributed to a couple of cretins wearing bath towels?''

"They're not towels,'' Remo explained, holding out the garments in his hands. "They're togas. The Roman senators used to wear them.''

"And people voted for them? Were they nudists?''

"Everybody wore them.''

"Who?'' Chiun demanded. "No self-respecting person would don such a degenerate-looking thing.''

"Lots of people did. Aristotle wore one.''

"Never heard of him,'' Chiun sniffed. "A charlatan.''

"He was one of the most famous philosophers of all time.''

"Did he speak of the beauty of the shores of Sinanju?''

"Well, not exactly. . . .''

"Then he is a charlatan. Everyone knows all true philosophers are Korean.''

"Okay,'' Remo sighed. He searched his mind for another toga wearer. "I've got it. Julius Caesar wore one. He was a great emperor.''

Chiun pouted. "Who cares what white men wear?"

"Just put it on. We can't get into the ceremony without them."

Reluctantly, Chiun took it from Remo's outstretched hands. "I will wear this shameful garment on one condition," he said.

"Yeah?" Remo asked hopefully. "What is it?"

"That you tell these fools gathered here that it was I who performed the double-spiral air blow that sent the two degenerate ones into the heavens."

"I can't do that. They'll turn against us. Right now they like us, so even Foxx can't throw us out. We've got to stick around to see what he's doing."

While Remo spoke, Chiun was swinging his head back and forth, his eyes closed, his jaw clamped shut with finality.

"Aw, come on, Chiun. It'll make things so much harder. And I want to be down there now, before Foxx makes his move."

"That is my condition."

"Anything else. Ask for anything else, and I'll do it. We can spend our next vacation in Sinanju, if you want it."

"We are spending our next vacation in Sinanju in any case," he said. "It is my turn to choose the yearly vacation, and I have already made my choice clear to Emperor Smith."

"Then how about a new Betamax?" Remo suggested. "I'll get you the whole setup, with a four-foot-wide screen and everything."

"I am content with such humble viewboxes as I already have," Chiun pronounced.

Remo gave up. "Isn't there anything you want badly enough to wear that toga for?" he asked in desperation.

Chiun was silent. Then a gleam came to the old almond-shaped eyes, and he spoke. "Perhaps there is one thing. One small thing."

"Here it comes. Okay, shoot."

"Bring me a picture of Cheeta Ching in ceremonial Korean robes. For this, will I cast aside my self-respect to appear publicly in a bathtowel. It will prove to her the extent of my admiration of her beauty."

Remo's mouth tasted sour at the thought of confronting the Ho Chi Minh of the airwaves. Still, it beat revealing to the patrons of Shangri-la that Chiun had nearly murdered two of their number over a passing thought. "You got it," he said.

"O wondrous day," Chiun cheeped happily as he wrapped the white toga around his yellow brocade robe. "Remember, you promised."

Remo grunted.

The banquet hall at Shangri-la was a sea of white togas and sparkling martini glasses. The chauffeur who had driven the guests from the train station at Enwood milled around the crowd, looking uncomfortable in his toga, passing out grotesque two-foot-tall Aztec masks.

"What's this for?" Remo asked as the chauffeur handed him a huge green and white mask.

"The pageant," the chauffeur said dourly as he passed on to the next guest.

"A play," Chiun explained. "It is like television." He placed his mask over his face with great ceremony. "O lovely one," he intoned, "when I behold your gracious ways. . ."

"Shhh," someone interjected as the lights dimmed and the figure of Felix Foxx, unmasked, stepped up to a dais on the far side of the room.

"Ladies and gentlemen," he began.

Chiun clapped wildly. "It is good to encourage actors," he said.

"We are gathered here tonight to partake of the miracle of Shangri-la. The stripping away of the years, the defiance of time, the triumph of youth and beauty are the province of the esteemed few who hear me now."

"Hear, hear," Chiun yelled.

Foxx looked into the darkened crowd, then continued: "As Coleridge wrote of the dreamer in his immortal poem *Kubla Khan*: 'Weave a circle 'round him thrice, and touch his eyes with holy dread, for he on honeydew has fed, and drunk the milk of Paradise.' In Shangri-la, we are all such dreamers, weaving our own magic circle, privileged to partake of the milk of Paradise ourselves. . . ."

"With a needle full of drugs from the body of a dead girl," Remo said to Chiun.

"Silence, unenlightened one," Chiun snapped. "He is a fine actor. Perhaps on the level with Rad Rex in 'As the Planet Revolves.' Not as good as Cheeta Ching."

"And so it is in this spirit of magic that we begin the Exit of Age. Will the players come forward?"

Foxx stepped off the dais. At the same moment, Chiun rushed forward, elbowing those in his way toward the far corners of the room as he stepped up on the platform.

"We will begin with an ode written by myself. It describes the sorrow of the Korean virgin Hsu T'ching after the passing of the warrior, Lo Pang, in the province of Katsuan during the reign of Ko Kang, regent of Wa Sing," Chiun said.

A low moan of dismay went up from the crowd as the players in the pageant tried to mount the dais and were pushed off by Chiun, who swatted them away like flies as he recited. Two men managed to mount the platform, and took Chiun by either arm. With a slight jerk Chiun sent them sprawling against the walls.

While everyone's eyes were on the crazy old Oriental on the stage, Remo was watching Felix Foxx on the right side of the room, near the archway into the small kitchen that served the guests in the ballroom. Ignoring the spectacle Chiun was creating on the dais, Foxx whispered something to the chauffeur. The chauffeur nodded. Remo didn't like the look on the chauffeur's face as he handed Foxx a huge red and black mask. He liked it even less when Foxx slipped out of the room.

Remo followed, pushing past the guests crowded into the dim amber-colored room, but by the time he reached the archway, Foxx had returned, a martini in his hand, his face covered by the mask. He recognized Remo with a cold nod and a brief uplifting of his glass. As Foxx wandered around the room, Remo's eyes never left him.

"And, lo, the wind, wild as the fury of the warrior's spear . . ."

"Couldn't we please get on with the pageant?" someone suggested.

Chiun sniffed contemptuously. "Lo, the wicked wind . . ."

Foxx was behind Remo. With his peripheral vision, Remo could trace the movements of the swaying white toga as it inched slowly around to the rear of the room until Foxx was directly behind him. Remo concentrated on his own feet, which would pick up the vibrations of footfalls through the floor. The ones he sensed were nearly balanced, but not quite. There was apprehension in them, an almost imperceptible haltingness. And he was carrying something. Nothing as heavy as a gun, but *something*, held in front of him so that his weight pitched slightly forward.

"Thus rode Lo Pang into Katsuan, wielding the horns of the antelope . . ." Chiun spoke.

And then the room was bathed in total darkness.

There was a stampede. There was panic and terror. But even before the first scream, Remo felt the man behind him pitch forward with the weapon in his hands, and Remo knew what it was while it still swooped overhead.

Wire.

It looped and sang downward, slicing through the air in front of Remo's face. He followed the momentum of the wire with his palms, jutting them forward and down to throw his assailant off balance. Remo kicked backward and connected with bone in a sickening, muffled crack, then used the leverage of his own position to toss the man overhead. To the accompaniment of frenzied shrieks, the man landed with a thud, half-way across the room.

A handful of people had pulled out cigarette lighters to illuminate the suddenly darkened room in dim, unconnected patches of light. Remo took one of the lighters and brought it close to the unmoving figure on the floor, his black and red mask at a crazy angle to his body.

Don't let him be dead, Remo thought in a rush of panic. If he'd killed Foxx, all his secrets would go with him. *I should have been more careful. I knew he was coming. I should have pulled back*. . . . He stripped off the mask. Beneath it, eyes open and glazed, a thin trickle of blood escaping from his mouth, was the lifeless face of Foxx's chauffeur.

"Chiun!" Remo called. But Chiun was already beside him, his face pressed against the outside wall.

"He is gone," the old man said. "The gates outside have closed."

"Gone?" someone screamed. "Foxx?"

Suddenly Remo was surrounded by people acting as if they were in a burning airplane. "What about the injections?" a man asked. "We'll miss the injections."

"Guess you'll just have to wait," Remo said irritably, trying to pull himself away from the grasping hands and loud wails of the guests.

"We can't wait," a woman sobbed. "We'll die. You don't understand. It has to be tomorrow." She was clutching Remo like a drowning person. "It'll be too late. We're dead. We're all dead."

"Aren't you all being a little dramatic?" Remo said, forcing his way toward the open door. Outside, Chiun was already making his way through the five-foot-high snowdrifts. "Please. I've got to go."

"No, don't go," she screamed. "You helped us before. You've got to help us now. Help us! You have to. You owe it to us!"

She struggled and squealed as a pair of hands pried her loose from Remo. In the darkness, Remo had to squint to see who his rescuer was.

It was Posie. She was smiling, a strange, sad smile. "Don't worry about us," she said.

"Do you know where he's going?" Remo asked.

She shook her head. "Wherever it is, he wants to be alone," she said with a sexy Mae West irony. "He's cut all the power lines and locked the outside gate. I've just checked the basement. The treatments for us are gone."

"I'm sorry, Posie," Remo said. "I guess the next few days are going to be rough for you. Without the drugs, I mean."

"It's okay," she said. She smiled, but her face had a hollow, frightened look. "He'll leave tracks that you can follow. That is, if you don't freeze to death. You have a terrific body, but I'd throw something over it besides that toga if I were you."

Remo looked down at the flowing white drape with embarrassment and tore it off. "Can you keep everybody under control here until I get back?"

"Sure," she said. "But don't bother hurrying back. You won't make it in time, anyway."

"What are you talking about?"

"Just get Foxx," Posie said. "He's the one who's responsible for what's going to happen here."

"Is everybody nuts?" Remo said. "You all act like some stupid injection is a matter of life and death."

He hesitated for a moment. Her face suddenly looked drawn and . . . *old*, Remo thought. But she smiled, and the image passed. Even at seventy, Posie Ponselle was a gorgeous creature.

"Just spoiled," she said winsomely. "Don't worry about us. We'll stay inside and tell ghost stories by candlelight." She touched his face. For a moment, he thought he saw that same impossible aged look creep over her stunning features. "Remo," she asked haltingly, "will you do something for me before you leave?"

"You don't have to ask," he said.

"Kiss me."

He held her close and pressed his lips to hers. The same electric warmth he had first felt with her surged through him again. "I'm going to miss you while I'm gone," he said.

She drew a manicured finger alongside his face. "I'll miss you, too. More than you know."

She let him go. Near the door, Seymour Burdich stood waiting, a down parka tossed ludicrously over his toga.

"I don't know what the hell's going on around here, but I'm going with you," he said, looking pale and trembling.

"Forget it," Remo said. "It's too cold, and you'd never be able to follow us, anyway."

"But it's spooky here," Burdich complained. "Everybody's crying bloody murder. There's something terrible happening. I want to help."

"There's nothing you can do. I didn't see a house or a gas station within twenty miles of here. Anyone who went out in this weather longer than ten minutes would freeze."

"You're going out"

"We're different," Remo said. "You just stay inside with the rest. I'll send help when I can."

Before he left, he looked back once more at Posie Ponselle. She was carrying two lit candles into the room from the kitchen. The firelight made her look, in her Grecian gown, like some pale and beautiful statue. He'd come close to loving her, and for that he would always owe her one. As he watched, she lifted her head in his direction. She smiled. At that moment, she was more beautiful than she'd ever been.

Her lips formed one word. "Good-bye," she said, and then she turned away.

We Interrupt This Book For a Message from Chiun

After all my warnings, you are still reading this nonsense?

Shame on you.

Have I not told you that those two paper-ruiners, Murphy and before him, that Sapir, get everything wrong? And if they do not get it wrong, then Pinnacle Books gets it wrong?

Don't you ever learn anything?

But at last, there is hope. I, Chiun, Master of Sinanju, have finally written a book of my own. It is called **The Assassin's Handbook,** and it tells the true story of the House of Sinanju and is filled with wonderful, exciting tales about such marvelous Masters as Wang the Greater. It includes my almost-favorite Ung poem and The Assassin's Quick Weight-Loss Diet and 37 Steps to Sexual Ecstasy.

There is a book inside the book that tells of the death of Remo, my student. Nowhere else will you read this true story.

Unfortunately, the book also has some junk in it, including a picture of Sapir and Murphy. But that is the price we artists must pay to bring beauty to a troubled world.

Buy my book. Buy one for a friend so that he too may appreciate the beauty of the real assassin.

You can get this book by filling out the little coupon below. The book costs $6.95. All the money will go to me. This is as it should be. I do all the work.

—Chiun

By his awesome hand in this 2,712th year of the dread Dragon Wind.

Chapter Ten

Chiun was already on the far side of the gate, the toga gone and replaced by the shimmering yellow of his long robe. The tire tracks from Foxx's Jeep traversed both sides of the gate and led off into the snow-drifted road beyond. There were no other vehicles on the grounds. Foxx, Remo realized, had seen to this eventuality long before.

Foxx's departure couldn't have been more advantageously timed. Five minutes after Remo vaulted over the ironwork gate at Shangri-la, the snow had started to fall; within another twenty minutes the tracks were all but obscured beneath the swirling snowstorm that raged all around them.

The cold was not a factor. Like a lizard, Remo had learned to adapt his body temperature to his environment. In the sixties, America's scientific community was stood on its ear when it was reported that Soviet cosmonauts had begun to learn control of their bodies to the point of lowering the temperature of their big toes at will. Remo could lower the temperature of his big toe in his sleep. Controlling his body temperature was as natural as breathing. He was beginning to achieve the stage in his development where he, like

Chiun, adapted to hot and cold automatically, with the same unthinking speed as a normal person's heartbeat slows when he's asleep.

So the cold meant nothing to Remo. The visibility was a different matter.

"I think we've had it," Remo said when they approached a fork in the road. Both tines of the fork were drifted knee-deep in fluffy banks of glistening snow. Beneath the starless, pitch-black expanse of sky, there was no such thing as a tire tread mark.

"Jokes, always jokes," Chiun grumbled, veering off to the left at a speed so fast that he barely cracked the surface of the new snow. "And not even good jokes at that. Learn to be funny before you make jokes. Old Korean proverb."

"I'm not joking. Hey, what makes you so sure he went left?" From the traces of Foxx and his jeep that remained, the man might as well have veered upward in a helicopter.

Chiun whirled around to face him, his almond eyes rounded in surprise. "You are asking me seriously how I knew? Do you not have a nose?"

"A *nose*?"

The old man lifted a handful of freshly fallen snow from the road. In his hand the snowflakes remained as they had been on the road, crystalline and unmelted. "Can you not smell it?"

Remo craned down to sniff at the snow. He hadn't been paying attention to his senses, concentrating instead on his lowered temperature and the extraordinary night vision necessary in the blinding storm. But when he pushed his concentration toward his olfactory membranes, he *did* smell something. High-octane gasoline, motor oil, rubber, and faint metallic traces from the underside of the vehicle. Altogether they existed in such small quantities that even an electron microscope might not have perceived the particles, but they were there, wafting through each new layer of snow.

"Oh, yeah," Remo said with some astonishment. "But I couldn't smell it from here, standing up." He felt ashamed as soon as he said it. His words had smacked of excuses.

He looked sheepishly at Chiun, but the old man only smiled. "That is why I am still the Master of Sinanju and you the pupil."

He was right, Remo thought as he followed the frail old Oriental through the snow. Chiun might act like a loony, but when it came down to it, he could still smell a droplet of motor oil beneath a foot of snow, standing at full height. He could still skim across the flakes with barely a footprint. And his double-spiral air blow had been pretty good, too.

"You're something, all right, Little Father," he said.

Chiun glanced back at him in surprise. For a moment, his face took on the look of a small child, immensely pleased. But it was the briefest hesitation, and the moment passed.

"Fool," he grumbled.

Foxx's jeep was parked, still steaming, at Graham Airport, a small, blue-lit compound some twelve miles outside of Enwood, consisting of a short airstrip, a cinderblock building, an air sock, and little else. Remo checked the car. The distributor had been dismantled. Foxx wasn't taking any chances with a possible tail.

Inside the cinderblock building the base operator, a fat man with a reedy, wheezing voice that sounded as if it were being squeezed through a concertina, looked surprised to see him. He was wearing a down vest colored neon orange, baggy brown trousers, and a hunting cap with the flaps down. When he breathed, steam billowed out of him like a chimney. He spent several minutes eyeing Chiun's satin brocade robe and Remo's short-sleeved T-shirt before catching what Remo was saying.

". . . chart or something?"

"What's that, boys?"

"I said, did the guy who just flew out of here leave any kind of a chart?"

The base op heaved himself out of his chair with a visible struggle and lumbered creakily toward a stained formica counter top, where a clipboard anchored by a paper cup full of cold and greasy coffee lay.

"Yeah. Right here," he said, holding the clipboard at arm's length and squinting. "Foxx, that the name?"

"That's him."

"Says here he filed for Deaver. Only Deaver's closed." He slapped the board back on the counter.

"What's a deaver?"

The fat man chuckled. "Guess you're not a flyer," he said. "Deaver's an airport. Near Clayton, South Dakota."

Suddenly Remo remembered the cases of procaine Posie said were being shipped regularly to South Dakota. "Is Deaver in the Black Hills?"

The base op wheezed out a sickly chortle. "That it is," he said, shaking his head. "That's some crazy pilot, flying out in this weather. For the Black Hills, yet. Hear it's near thirty below there. Snow up to your waist. I told him, but these flyboys'll do anything with a lick or two of whiskey in 'em." He shrugged. "It's his plane, I guess."

"We've got to get over there," Remo said. "Is there a pilot who can take us anywhere near Deaver airport?"

The base op's wheezing chuckle blossomed into a mirthful roar, his belly rolling. "Listen, son. There isn't a pilot in the country'll fly you out of this. And most of South Dakota's so bad, nothing but a penguin's got a chance out there. I told that Foxx fella Deaver's closed and he'd have to land somewheres in a field or something, most likely, but he gone on ahead anyway. Hate to say it, but I won't be surprised if he don't make it." He touched Remo lightly on the shoulder. "Take my advice, son. Stay inside. Whatever bravery you been drinkin' or smokin' that got you to come out here in that tee-shirt's going to give you a good case of pneumonia 'fore long. Go home." There was compassion in his eyes, kindly eyes that had watched a hundred good pilots flame out in the air and hurtle to their deaths in moments of youthful impulsiveness.

Suddenly Remo remembered the guests at Shangri-la. "Can I use your phone?" he asked. "There are some people stuck in a house near here with no phones and no electricity. I want to call the police."

The base op wheezed. "You city boys're always panicking. Electricity goes out all the time in these parts. And the phones are down all over. The one here ain't working, neither."

"But you've got a radio or something, haven't you?" Remo persisted. "Foxx made his flight plans with somebody."

"The FAA don't take kindly to using the radio for a thing like this. And they ain't no cops, anyway, can get out here tonight. Your friends're going to be just fine, son. Just snowed in a while. Their phones'll be work-

ing in the morning, same as mine. I'll call the police
then, if you want, but they'll probably beat me to it
themselves."

"But the lines were *cut,*" Remo explained. "And
everybody at Shangri-la was acting like they were
going to die. . . ."

The base op huffed disdainfully. "You talking about
that fancy place up the road?" He made a rude gesture. "Bunch of spoiled city folks, that's what they are.
Used to having everything they want, more'n likely. I
heard they was all dope fiends, anyway."

Maybe the man was right, Remo thought. Maybe
the hysterical doomsaying of the guests at the clinic
was no more than the whining of a bunch of spoiled
brats used to having their every whim satisfied immediately. "Okay," he said to the base op. He gave the
address of the house called Shangri-la. "I suppose it
can wait till morning."

He would set things right as soon as he could. If he
could find a phone that worked tonight, he would call
Smitty. Smitty would take care of notifying the police
about the people at Shangri-la. For the time being,
though, he had to find Foxx.

"Hey, look out there!" the base op called in alarm.

Chiun, who hadn't been paying any attention to the
exchange between Remo and the base op, was over
by the door of the cinderblock building, raptly poking
and prodding a rackful of skis. One of the bolts had
come loose, and the skis were dangling precariously.
With one tug, Chiun forced one of them out of the rack
and sent the rest clattering to the floor.

"A strange utensil indeed," he remarked, in-
specting the smooth polished wood of the ski.

"Now just a second there, old timer." the base op
said, his rotund face clouding. "It took me near half

a day to set up that there rack. I need those skis."

"I'll pay for any damage," Remo said quickly. The germ of an idea was growing. "Say, what do you use these for, anyway?"

The base op lumbered darkly toward the pile of skis and inspected them. "These here are cross-country skis," he said. "I come to work in 'em. My old clunker Olds wouldn't make it out here in this weather if I filled her full of diamonds. Keep some extra pairs around in case somebody needs 'em. Out here we're used to bad winters." He was puffing and grunting as he bent over to inspect the fallen rack. "Well, no harm done, I 'spect. Just a hell of a lot of trouble to stick this thing back up." He waddled slowly back to the counter, where he produced a hammer and rummaged for nails.

"No problem," Remo said. He located the fallen nails on the floor, aligned the rack with the holes in the wall, and pressed the nails back into place. By the time the base op arrived with his tools, the rack was repaired.

"Well, that was mighty nice of you," he said, his face regaining its kindliness. "How'd you do that so fast?"

"It was nothing," Chiun said.

"I'd like to buy a couple of pairs from you," Remo said.

The base op laughed. "You planning on skiing to South Dakota?"

"Maybe," Remo said. "I'll give you a thousand dollars for two pairs." He pulled out his wallet.

The base op blinked with surprise. "That's a pretty nice piece of change, boy."

"It's worth it to me. Will you take it?"

"Well, I don't know . . . I don't feel right sending

you and the old fella out in the weather like this. Why don't you wait till the storm breaks? I'll get a good pilot to fly you over to Deaver in the morning."

"I can't wait till morning," Remo said. "Is it a deal?"

"Well . . ." After some thought, the base op reached out and took the bills. "It still don't seem right," he said. But Remo was already fitting the skis onto Chiun's tiny feet.

The old man grinned ecstatically. "Skates," he said, his eyes sparkling.

"Skis. We'll cover ground faster than we could on foot."

The base op held up a pudgy hand. "No, I know this is a free country and all, but traveling to South Dakota on skis is just plain ridic'lous. I can't stop you from kill-ing yourself, sonny, but you got to think of the old fella here. He'll never make it."

Chiun stood up, wobbled for a second, then clapped to the door. "How do they work?" he asked, obviously thrilled with his new toy.

"You've got to push yourself along with these," Remo said, holding up a pair of poles. But it was too late. Chiun was already out the door and picking up speed fast, sliding around the small building at eight revolutions a minute.

"Got to hand it to him. The old guy's got a natural talent," the base op said, bewildered.

Past the runway lights they watched Chiun speed toward a high drift. He skimmed the top of it with barely a mark and sailed skyward, clearing a high pine. He was cackling exultantly.

"I don't think you have to worry about him," Remo said.

Chapter Eleven

Seymour Burdich set down the crowbar and moved his fingers to get some feeling back into them. He stood knee-deep in snow at the locked iron gate to Shangri-la. Through the swirling snowstorm he could barely make out the dark outline of the mansion.

They were in there, all the Beautiful People who made the world go round, only they weren't beautiful now. They were screaming and shivering in helpless terror over the thought that their guru, Dr. Foxx, had abandoned them. Like children, Burdich thought, blowing on his hands. He'd managed, in the hour or so that he'd been outside, to pry open two of the bars, nearly wide enough to squeeze through. He picked up the crowbar and went to work again.

He was going to be a hero for this. The thought warmed him a hundred times more than the old kerosene lamp that glowed dully beside the ironwork of the gate. Heroes were immediately accepted with that group. Look at Remo. He wasn't even a member, and they'd let him stay on. *Because he was a hero*.

God knew he was the only one in that crowd, although, he had to admit, Posie Ponselle was okay. She'd at least kept her wits about her. Posie pulled out blankets and organized a team to keep the fireplaces going and brewed coffee over the open fire in the banquet hall and played the piano. Also, she'd talked the group into changing out of those ridiculous togas they were wearing and into party clothes. That was just like Posie, turning a nightmare into a party.

She was okay. Burdich would do a special writeup on her in the *Celebrity Scoop* when he got back to New York. But the rest of them were completely out of it, screaming their heads off about the end of the world and dying of old age and all kinds of crazy nonsense. A bunch of babies, that's what they were. Some Beautiful People. All the guts of a playground full of kindergartners.

And to think that he'd agonized for twenty years about not having the scratch to join them at their precious Shangri-la. What a crock. When it came right down to it, no one had even volunteered to help him pry open the gate. They'd all said they were too old.

He'd laughed secretly to himself at that one. Here were the *crème de la crème,* the chosen few who, like Coleridge's dreamer in the poem Foxx read at the ceremony, had entered the magic circle of eternal youth. Here were people who had drunk the milk of Paradise every month since before the Flood, practically, until every one of them looked twenty years younger than he did, and they were all moaning that they were too *old.* Crybabies.

The weird thing was, when Burdich looked at them in the firelight before he left the house, they *did,* look old. It was scary. Even Posie Ponselle, easily one of the great beauties of all time, was starting to look haggard. There was something around her eyes and mouth. It wasn't right there on the surface—she was still a knockout—but it seemed to lie just beneath her skin, something that was trying to come through, something . . . *decayed*.

Burdich shook his head to clear it. It was just his imagination. Posie was tired, that was all. That went for all of them. Tired and hysterical. And it went triple for Burdich. He was half frozen already, and he hadn't even made it out of the gate yet.

But it would be worth it. Once he came back with the cops, all the rich nobs at Shangri-la would give him a hero's welcome. He wouldn't be—what did Remo call him?—a mascot. He wouldn't be their mascot anymore, tolerated at their highbrow parties because he was mildly helpful to them. No more. After he saved their rich butts, they would take him into their hearts without reservation. He would be one of them. He would belong.

Still, at the moment, Burdich's forthcoming triumph seemed empty. Shangri-la, for all its illustrious clients, was a weird place, and he'd come out into the cold as much to get away from it as to perform his heroic act. He wanted to help them, yes. He wanted to be their savior, their champion. But mostly he wanted to get as far away from that dark house full of screaming half-ghosts as he could.

With one last, back-wrenching tug that pulled his shirt and his undershirt out of his pants so that his back was exposed to the stinging waves of snow, the bars squeaked open the last centimeter or so necessary to let him out. He pressed himself through the bars, feeling as if he were going through a spaghetti machine, grateful that he hadn't put on much weight through the years. Keeping his boyish figure had been mostly a function of being stone broke most of the time, but it had finally been of some use. He pulled the flickering kerosene lamp out after him and started the long hike toward . . .

Toward what? He hadn't seen so much as a birdhouse on the way out. But there had to be someplace. This was Pennsylvania, not the Himalayas. Someone had to live around here.

He trudged off through the trackless, snow-covered road, squinting to see five feet in front of him. The decision to leave Shangri-la had been the right one, he knew. He could feel it. Just outside the gates the air seemed sweeter, somehow, more alive. Inside, with the guests at the mansion, it hadn't smelled good. There was something stale and putrid there.

Suddenly the image of Posie Ponselle's face came to him again. *Something decayed, just below the surface. . . .* He felt ashamed for thinking about her that way. Posie was a good egg, the best of the lot. Still there was something about her that reminded Burdich of the stink of a beggar.

Then, with swift, blinding clarity, Burdich knew what it was in that house that he had feared so much that he was willing to walk all night in a raging blizzard to escape. It was death. He knew it as surely as he knew it was snowing. When those wild-eyed nobs in there were screaming about dying, they weren't just whistling Dixie. Death crouched in that house like a dog waiting for scraps.

He walked for what he guessed was a half-hour or more, although it could have been longer or no more than a few minutes. He couldn't tell. His brain had numbed along with his fingers and toes and the ice cube on his face that had once been his nose. Posie's face (just below the surface) kept occurring to him (death crouched in the corners, stinking like a beggar), but he tried to blot that out of his mind and concentrate on his steps, one foot in front of the other.

His eyelashes were frozen into sparkling spikes. They gave off brilliant flashes whenever he blinked, and that was a nice diversion. One foot in front of the other. His steps were growing shorter, since his legs had numbed with the cold. He had long since stopped rubbing his hands together to introduce some feeling into them. The last time he'd tried that, over the kerosene lamp, he'd burned off a patch of skin the size of a half-dollar on the backs of his hands, before the lamp had flickered and then gone out—and he hadn't even felt it.

(Death crouched.)

And his eyelashes! Jesus, they must weigh a ton. So hard to raise them more than a slot. . . . A slit, a slot, a happy thought. . . . His brain was dancing. The *Celebrity Scoop* was on the presses, banging away to tell the world about Jackie O's new man and "LIZA'S NERVOUS BREAKDOWN," as the headline would read, only to clear itself in the text, by saying she wasn't suffering any such thing, but by then Liza's fans will have already bought the *Scoop,* so it didn't matter. The *Celebrity Scoop* was running, and the front pages were shuffling out into the stacker, and all the stars were on it, the Beautiful People, and his picture was there, too, big as life. SEYMOUR BURDICH, BEAUTIFUL AT LAST.

"Beautiful People," Burdich sang in a thin, shaky voice to the tune of "Beautiful Dreamer." "Wake unto me. . . ."

Had to stay awake. He was in the middle of nowhere and (something) sat crouched and waiting. But it wouldn't touch him. He was the Beautiful Dreamer. Weave a circle 'round him thrice, and touch his eyes . . .

His eyes were sealing shut. The icicle eyelashes, the swollen frostbite on his eyelids, the terrible, aching desire for sleep made him close them, and it didn't matter, he was still on his feet, he would just rest his eyes (touch his eyes with holy dread) for a moment and keep on walking, the important thing was to keep on walking, go ahead, you're not going to meet anybody along this road, Beautiful Dreamer.

"For he on honeydew has fed," Burdich shouted into the night, his voice a rasp that the wind caught and smashed almost before the words were out of his mouth. Keep walking. You're not going to meet anybody.

But he did.

With an effort, he opened his frozen eyes and saw that he had wandered into a cluster of trees on the edge of a deep pine forest. Where was the road? He was hip-deep in snow, leaning against the trunk of a sturdy blue spruce. And there he saw him, *Him,* in the same cluster of trees. Crouching. Waiting.

"You've been looking for me all along, haven't you?" Burdich said in a low whisper that hurt his lungs.

He sat down in the snow. It felt so good. Eyes so tired (touch his eyes with holy dread). And as Death wove its circle around him, Burdich smiled, his lips barely moving as he repeated the last lines of the poem. "For he on honeydew has fed . . ." It was going to be all right now. Death wouldn't stay long here. It had another appointment, up the road, with a houseful of people who expected him.

"And drunk the milk of Paradise," he whispered.

He didn't have the strength to close his eyes, so the snow swirled in and filled in the open slots and blanketed him in brilliant white.

And then Death went on up the road.

Chapter Twelve

In Washington, D.C., some 280 miles due southeast of the cluster of pines where Seymour Burdich's corpse lay blanketed with snow, Secretary of the Army Clive R. Dobbins sat in the back seat of his dark blue Lincoln Mark V, surreptitiously peering at his wristwatch as his wife prattled on with a thousand complaints.

"Really, Clive, I can't see why we had to leave so early. It was a simply fabulous party. Nancy even gave me her recipe for that scrumptious Charlotte Russe she makes. And Henry was in marvelous spirits."

"The snow," Dobbins said lamely. Washington hadn't been hit very hard by the snowstorm that was sweeping the country, but the weather made a better story than the truth.

"What?" Mrs. Dobbins registered a surprise greater than any she could have felt, but exaggeration was part of her personality, so Dobbins let her go on. "There aren't two inches of snow on the ground, dear. And Forsythe is an utterly splendid driver. Aren't you, Forsythe?"

"Yes, ma'am," the driver agreed from the front seat.

131

"I've got to make a meeting," Dobbins muttered. Which was true. The meeting was with a twenty-four-year-old public relations girl with the State Department. Rhonda had the brains of a duck, but a rack on her that could halt an ICBM coming out of its silo.

Dobbins had told her he'd meet her at one A.M. on the nose, and he was twenty minutes late already. It would take another half-hour or so to get from Georgetown to Rhonda's section of Sixteenth Avenue. She was never much good if he dropped by while she was sleeping. The girl slept like a rock. Fooling around with Rhonda after waking her up was like diddling a mummy.

"Step on it, Forsythe," he said.

Out of the rear window he could see the headlights of the green Ford belonging to the Secret Service. They followed him everywhere like shadows. Dobbins had objected to their presence ever since the boys had first started to trail him around, but the order was from the president himself, and you didn't buck orders like that.

So he had put up with their bothersome lurking and checking, even though it made him feel like a pansy. He'd commanded men in three wars, damn it, and now a bunch of civies who looked like college frat men were fluttering around him like butterflies in order to "protect" him.

Protect! Hah! He'd like to see the son of a bitch who popped off Watson and Ives. He'd like to see the whites of that pud-puller's eyes as he tried to attack him, a retired four-star general of the United States Army, because if he did attack him, Dobbins's clenched fist going smack into that yellow-bellied turd-eater's nose would be the last sight the so-called assassin was ever going to see.

The big car rambled into Georgetown, passing by the elegant houses with their covered pools and their steaming greenhouses. Behind it, the green Ford followed doggedly.

"Punks," Dobbins muttered.

"What, dear?" Mrs. Dobbins said, her false eyelashes batting so fast she looked about to lift off. "Now you know how I feel about your getting overexcited, Clive. You know, I've always held that you play much too much golf."

"I don't golf in the winter, Hilda."

"Don't you?" Again the look of unbridled amazement. "Well, work then. You spend altogether too much of your time working. All these meetings." She clucked disapprovingly.

"I'm the Secretary of the Army," Dobbins said mildly.

"But it's past midnight. Surely the Russians wouldn't be so uncivilized as to attack us before breakfast."

Dobbins sighed and tuned out the rest of Hilda's monologue. At least Rhonda limited her talking to smut. He liked that in a woman. No wasted words. Hilda was still jabbering when the Lincoln pulled up in front of the three-story Tudor with "Dobbins" printed over the bell. She hardly seemed to notice when Dobbins led her out of the car and into the house; the verbal river that flowed from her lips never ceased. She was still talking when he closed the door behind her and headed back out to the car.

"Get out, Forsythe," he snapped.

"Sir?"

"Quick, before the Secret Service boys get here." They were undoubtedly nearby, cooling their well-bred heels inconspicuously somewhere near the entrance to Dobbins's driveway, but it was worth a shot. "Give me your hat."

The driver, clearly put out, climbed reluctantly out of the car. "Sir, I was given instructions—"

"Damn it, I'm your employer, and I give the instructions around here!"

"Yes, sir." He handed Dobbins the navy blue chauffeur's cap he wore. Dobbins grunted in acknowledgment and squeezed in behind the wheel. "You go home now, hear?"

"Yes, sir," Forsythe said dejectedly.

Dobbins pulled out of the driveway slowly, then laid rubber heading for 34th Avenue. Headlights were behind him. Oh, the boys are on their toes tonight, he thought. But not for long. He jumped one red light, gassed the car hard, and sped up Wisconsin Avenue. The lights were still tailing him.

"Here we go, kids. Earn your pay," he said out loud, grinning as he pushed the Lincoln as fast as it would go up onto the ramp leading to Connecticut Avenue and along the Potomac.

No peach-fuzzed protectors were going to hang around spying on Clive R. Dobbins, he thought triumphantly as he gunned along the snow-slicked highway toward Bethesda. His personal life was his own, and if he was going to bang Rhonda behind his wife's back, nobody was getting in on that action except for him and for Rhonda, if she was awake, and the souls on Judgment Day. Certainly no flab-headed civilians in a Ford.

The river sped by alongside, the cold moonlight glinting off the water and bringing up the dull-white shapes of the ice floes that regularly dammed up the river at this time of year. There was some traffic, not much. What there was, was inching along at a snail's pace, while Dobbins sped past them like a black bullet. He was ahead of all of them.

He checked his rear-view. Not all of them. There was one pair of headlights behind him, going at his pace, no slower, no faster.

Dobbins cursed under his breath. Those Fords had to be built with Maserati engines in them. Well, it was going to take more than a hot engine and a car full of youngsters just barely off the tit to catch him.

"Try and follow this, you suckers!" he shouted as he spun into the inside lane. With one momentous burst of power, he jumped the median strip and headed full speed in the other direction.

"A trick, boys," he roared, coughing with laughter. They must have been asses to think he was going to Bethesda in the first place, Dobbins thought. Who screws in Bethesda, anyway?

Out of his rear-view he watched the green Ford skid and spin out into an uncontrollable donut across four lanes of traffic. It hit two vehicles superficially while sliding toward the far side of Connecticut Avenue. Several cars braked behind it, sending them into herringbone patterns along the roadway. The green Ford crashed into a guardrail and at last lay still.

Dobbins hooted with delight. It was clear sailing now. He put the car on cruise control at 60 and glided down Connecticut Avenue back toward the city. His thoughts filled with Rhonda. Rhonda, in a transparent pink negligee, with maybe the black garter belt he'd given her for Valentine's Day underneath. Rhonda of the deliciously foul mouth who knew just how to bring his wildest fantasies to life. Rhonda . . . if Rhonda was awake. Otherwise, he might as well be at home with Hilda. He cut the cruise control and gunned the pedal.

Back in the city, he made his way toward the north-

east section of town. Traffic was light and he made
good time. He didn't notice until he'd reached Sixteenth Avenue that the same headlights had been behind him since the crackup on the highway.

Damn it, if it wasn't the Secret Service boys, it was
the turd-eating reporters. Although no official word
about the assassinations of the secretaries of the Air
Force and the Navy had been given, the press boys
had noticed the added security around Dobbins and
took every opportunity to grill him about it. Ever since
the advent of the Secret Service guards, he'd denied
all press interviews and eschewed them with a hurried
"No comment" when they ran up to him on the street.

Oh, that's all I need, Dobbins thought as he
checked the rear-view again. It certainly looked like a
tail. The crud-mongers. He could just see the headlines now: "ARMY HEAD ELUDES SECURITY TO
RENDEZVOUS WITH WASHINGTON MISTRESS."
And there would be a picture next to it of Rhonda in
her flamingo-pink negligee with the black garter belt
underneath. Read all about it in the Pentagon Report.
Details in Clive R. Dobbins's dishonorable discharge
papers.

"Get off my ass, you wang-wavers!" he shouted as
he turned into a narrow sidestreet. He slowed down at
the entrance to an alley. If it wasn't a tail, the car that
had been driving behind him for the past twenty minutes would pass by harmlessly.

But it didn't. It turned into the same side street with
a deliberation that sent a sudden involuntary chill
down Dobbins's spine. He entered the alleyway, rolling slowly to avoid the stacks of piled-up garbage on
either side. Then he turned onto another side street.
And after that, another alley.

The car was still behind him.

Rhonda's plush apartment building was less than two blocks away. If he was going to get his portrait snapped, it sure as hell wasn't going to be in front of that building. He ground the Lincoln to a halt.

Fine. Snap away, boys. Think you're so damned smart. The only picture you're getting of me is going to be right here in this alley, while I give you the news that my lawyer's going to slap a harassment suit against your muckraking paper.

Stick that in your turd-eating notepads.

He got out slowly and walked toward the car behind him with kingly grandeur. They were going to see who's boss around here, by God. The car was a nondescript Chevy, as battered and dented as every other car in Washington. Something was poking out of the driver's window. In the darkness of the alley, Dobbins guessed it was the ubiquitous press credentials, which reporters seemed to think gave them access to every skeleton-filled closet in America. Well, he'd show them where they could stow their toe-sucking press cards.

Only it wasn't a press card. And the boys inside weren't jumping out like hyenas with their questions and their flashbulbs. Dobbins frowned as he moved closer, hearing nothing but the gritty sound of his own footfalls on the dirt and snow-covered brick of the alleyway. They certainly didn't act like any Washington reporters he ever saw.

Rookies, probably. Independents. Trying to get their first big public exposé, and not knowing a donkey's fart about how to get it. Well, here's your scoop, boys. And the subpoena will come in the morning to verify it. He pulled himself up to full height. He jutted an accusing finger at the car to throw a little scare into them. He put on his most authoritative general's voice. "What the hell are—"

The words choked off as the dark object poking through the driver's window lengthened and another, just like it, elongated sleekly out the rear window. And then he knew what they were as the men in the car— *what were they wearing?*—raised them to their shoulders and sighted through them and then the things bellowed bright fireworks in a deafening crash that sent brick flying off the walls behind Dobbins, and the general gasped once in red bubbles of blood, and his feet splayed out beneath him and the car was gone.

As he lay in the alleyway, riddled with what would later be determined as more than 100 wounds delivered from a Chinese copy of a Soviet AK-47 submachine gun at point-blank range, Clive R. Dobbins's last thought was that the Secret Service boys could never have stopped the men in that car. The president himself couldn't have stopped them, just as the president wouldn't be able to stop them the next time.

And the next time was going to be worse. Much worse.

Chapter Thirteen

DESTINATION ZADNIA.

The Folcroft computers spewed out another piece to the puzzle of Felix Foxx. Dawn was peeking in through the venetian blinds of Smith's office, and the light stung his eyes. He'd stayed awake in his office for two nights now, trying to sort out the tangled mess the computers had brought to him.

It was all there, he knew. Somewhere. During the past 48 hours the Folcroft Four had given him a million pieces of information. In Smith's weary brain, he began to see the trusted computers as four diabolically wise beings from some unearthly plane, who gave him all the parts to a machine and then said with a wink, "Okay, Smitty. Now you make it run."

But he hadn't been able to make it run. A hundred times over Smith had written down the salient points of the case. The overflowing wastebasket full of scraps of paper were testimony to his efforts. But nothing had jelled. The parts of the machine were as disparate as oranges and apples. With a sigh, he drew out another sheet of notepaper and began again.

First, there were the murders of the Secretary of the Air Force, Homer Watson, and the Secretary of the

Navy, Thornton Ives, both killed in strange ways that
reflected combat conditions. Every branch of the military had launched full-scale investigations on their
own, without turning up so much as the smell of a
lead. CURE's own man, Remo, had come up almost
as empty-handed. The only thing Remo had locked
onto was some middle-aged diet doctor named Foxx
who, for some unknown reason, the computers had
decreed to be a ninety-four-year-old man named Vaux
who was last heard from some fifty years before in
connection with a scandal involving the youth-re-
storing properties of a drug called procaine.

"2," Smith wrote neatly. Point Two was that Foxx/
Vaux had last been seen in the company of a woman
who was found murdered, her body drained of what
might have been an unusually high level of procaine.
The New York police were after Foxx on that one, but
they were looking in the wrong places. Foxx was at a
so-called aging clinic in Pennsylvania called
Shangri-la with Remo, and Smith wasn't about to turn
the information over to standard law enforcement
agencies until Remo had found what he had gone
after.

Shangri-la was Point Three. Apparently this was no
ordinary massage-and-mud-bath resort. Remo had reported guests to the clinic, who were in their seven-
ties, even though they looked barely old enough to
buy a drink. The procaine connection. Large amounts
of the drug might keep them young. At least that was
the theory advanced by Vaux in the thirties before he
disappeared off the face of the earth. That would explain Foxx/Vaux's advanced age, but little more. So
far, there was nothing to connect the strange goings
on with the two military murders.

Secret Service guards had been posted around

Clive R. Dobbins, the secretary of the Army, since he was the next logical choice for an assassination team bent on eliminating the country's military leaders, but if the hit team got through the Secret Service to Dobbins, who would be next? The Folcroft Four had answered with chilling efficiency, flashing the names of the next three possible victims: the secretary of Defense, the Secretary of State, and the president of the United States.

Time was running out. It was still eminently possible that Felix Foxx, for all the interesting revelations about him, had nothing to do with any murders except for that of the girl in New York City, and even that lead was circumstantial at best. Remo might have been on the wrong track all along. In the interests of time, Smith was on the verge of pulling Remo out of Shangri-la and having him start over.

And then, at 4:51 A.M., Smith wheeled Point Four out of the computers. Point Four was DESTINATION ZADNIA, and the words were printed on the console screen four times. Foxx, under the name of Felix Vaux, had traveled to Zadnia three times during the past year, and purchased an open ticket to the same place two months before.

That was the stickler. Why would a nationally celebrated diet doctor want to make four unpublicized visits to an unstable country in the north of Africa? Zadnia had nothing—no technology, no arable land, not even enough overweight people to fill one of Foxx's lectures. All Zadnia possessed was a power-mad dictator named Ruomid Halaffa who would buy arms and secrets from any source at any time in order to fuel, indiscriminately, the terrorist forces of the world. That and just enough oil to buy Halaffa's weapons from the lowest bidder.

"Zadnia," Smith said, bewildered. Across from him, the Folcroft Four seemed to be smirking. The last of the machine's parts had been handed over. *Now you make it run*.

He would have to call Remo. Maybe Remo had discovered somehting during the night that would shed some light on this Zadnia business. He called the Shangri-la number. The line was dead. No ring, nothing. He called the operator and asked her to dial the number for him. She told him that the line was out of order, possibly because of some violent snowstorms going on in that part of the country.

While the operator was talking, the special red phone on his desk, the one with the direct hookup to the president, rang. He immediately hung up on the operator and picked up the red phone on the first ring.

"Yes, Mr. President," he said. He listened for several minutes while the president spoke, and during those minutes Smith felt as if he'd aged five years. He could almost feel the flesh of his face sagging with each dreadful word on the other end of the line.

"Thank you for the information, Mr. President. We're working on it," he said and broke the connection.

Dobbins was dead. The killers had won again.

There was only one thing to do. Smith checked the special portable phone in his attaché case and locked the clasps. Then he memorized the coordinates of Shangri-la, which Remo had given him, pulled on his galoshes and coat, anf fixed his brown felt hat on his head. There was no time to wait for snowstorms. If Remo couldn't get out of Shangri-la, Smith would go there himself.

Chapter Fourteen

As Harold Smith was closing the catches to his attaché case, Remo was sitting in a pine lean-to somewhere in the Black Hills of South Dakota.

He should have known that Chiun would get bored with his new toy before they had gone even forty miles on their skis. But that had put them on a drivable main highway, and a truck driver had barreled them into Chicago.

Chicago itself, despite the arctic winds off Lake Michigan, was a blessing. O'Hare Airport was used to terrible weather and they managed to catch a flight as far as Sioux Falls, South Dakota.

Naturally, Chiun insisted on sitting in the seat next to the left wing, which was occupied by a Chinese widow who was nearly as boisterous as Chiun. After twenty minutes of mutual castigation, the rest of the passengers had demanded that both the strange old skinny Chinese guy and his wife be bodily ejected from the aircraft. Chiun made the point that he was neither Chinese nor crazy, which was what any person married to the Chinese lady would have to be in order to tolerate her dog-eating ways. He emphasized the point by knocking out the window above the left wing seat, causing the 727 to fall into a shrieking spin as oxygen masks dropped into the fusilage and several loose articles of clothing got sucked out into the atmosphere. The temperature inside the plane plummeted.

The plane climbed out of the spin only after Remo managed to stop up the open window with someone's red American Tourister weekender, which had heretofore not been collapsible. Then he'd had to give all three stewardesses a good sample of the 52 steps to ecstasy before they would agree that the missing window was a quirk of fate.

At Sioux Falls, Remo stole the first available automobile, a pink 1963 Nash Rambler, which puttered as far as Belvidere in Jackson County before giving up the ghost in a cloud of greasy black smoke. He'd kept the owner's registration card so that whoever usually drove the old fossil could be reimbursed. Smitty was going to love that. In his book, stealing cars was definitely not a desirable function of CURE, and paying for them was even less so.

They still had twenty miles to hike before even arriving in the right county, then eighty more skimming the 2,000-foot high cliffs of the South Dakota Badlands in the back seat of a souped-up '55 driven by suicidal teen-agers, before reaching Deaver Airport. Which, as the man said, was closed. A wonderful trip.

Now he sat under the pine lean-to, watching the morning sun blaze in full glory, while he wondered what to do next. The storm had quit about an hour after dawn, and the snow glistened, trackless, on the ground around him. A few feet away, Chiun slept quietly on a mat fashioned from twigs.

Chiun had led them to this spot in the middle of nowhere, based on nothing more than the fact that the area they were in was the least inhabited. Remo tried to argue that Felix Foxx was even less prepared than they were to brave the desolate countryside alone during a snowstorm, but Chiun had insisted. He heard echoes, he said. And, actually, Remo had heard them, away—faraway, disconnected echoes through the mountains that seemed to have no point of origin. But by that time he was too exhausted to know whether the echoes were anything more than the soughing of the wind in the trees.

Once they made camp, Chiun had slept immediately. The most Remo could do was to lower his heartrate and will his body into a simulation of basal metabolism. It was fake sleep, with all his senses keenly aware, but he had felt a little better afterward.

Suddenly Chiun sat up, bolt upright, his head cocked. Remo opened his mouth to speak, but the old man held up a restraining hand. He listened for a few more seconds, then said, "Prepare."

Remo heard it too. He burst out of the pine lean-to like an explosion.

There were six of them, very young, armed to the teeth and in uniform. *American Army uniforms*, Remo thought, although the garments didn't look much like the combat fatigue he remembered from Vietnam in his pre-CURE days. There was something strange about the lot of them, something bizarre yet familiar. It was a feeling. . . . No, a *smell*. A smell that reminded REMO of death and decay and falseness.

Chiun took out two of the soldiers at once with a twisting kick that sent them splattering against the trunks of two huge trees. REMO caught one of the men, a handsome youth of nineteen or twenty, in the solar plexus. Then he let fly with a right that wedged the fourth soldier's nose inside his brain.

It happened in a flash; four men were dead before the other two could even register what was going on. Here were two civilians, one a five-foot-tall Oriental about a hundred years old and the other a lunatic who slept outdoors in twelve-degree weather in a T-shirt, and they were obliterating the Team.

The Team, Sergeant Randall Riley thought as he saw the old Oriental circling with Davenport. Davenport was one of the Team. Like the other Team members, Davenport was unbeatable. Davenport was the best thing with a knife since Geronimo. That was why Foxx had recruited him. Davenport's prowess with a knife was too good for the regular army.

The army was an organization that told you to go out and kill, and when you killed they gave you medals and called you a hero. Until the war ended . And once it ended, you didn't get any more medals for killing. Oh, no. Suddenly, with the signing of a piece of paper, good knife men like Davenport weren't allowed to kill anymore. Suddenly there were rules that said that if you killed, you got martialed and thrown in the slammer till the worms ate out your eyes.

That was what the regular army did to Davenport. He'd still be rotting away in prison, his knife-arm used for making wallets, if it hadn't been for Foxx.

And the Team.

And now the Team was down by four, and this crazy old chink was taking on Davenport and his Bowie with his bare hands. Riley cocked the safety off his S & W Centennial Airweight and waited. Let Davenport have his fun with the old fool. Then he'd polish off the skinny guy with the Centennial.

For the Team.

He watched as Chiun and Davenport circled one another, Davenport's Bowie knife swiping the air savagely. The old man barely seemed to move, and yet each time the knife slashed downward to where the old man's face was, or his chest, or his belly, the old man was somehow gone from the spot.

Riley blinked. His eyes must not be working right, he decided. And then Davenport was on the gook, right, on top of him, and the knife was singing through the still morning air and shining in the bright morning sun, and then. . . . It wasn't possible! The knife was sailing over the tops of the trees, traveling like it had been shot out of a cannon, and attached to it was something pale and long with one end red and ragged that spilled a rain of blood. And then Davenport was screaming and his eyes were rolling like the eyes of a shot horse and he was pointing to the bloodied stump that used to be his shoulder and, Christ, it was just like Guadalcanal all over again, with men moaning while their arms and legs rolled like broken toys down the hills around them, oh, *Christ*!

Riley opened fire. A blur came toward him, and then he screamed as the bullet aimed for the thin man in the T-shirt missed and exploded into Davenport's guts. But by then the Centennial was somehow out of his hand, anyway, and there was nothing to do but run.

The Team. Got to tell the rest of the Team, Riley told himself, his thoughts blurred with the urine smell of fear that he hadn't known since the first days of World War II. Just running was a victory. He would never have even gotten the chance to run if he hadn't fallen down the twenty-foot cliff. The skinny guy in the T-shirt already had his hands on him after he'd knocked the Centennial out of his hand. Fortunately, the skinny guy only had hold of the cuff of Riley's trousers, and when Riley skidded off the edge and down the snow-covered drop, the fabric had torn. So now half of Riley's right pantleg was torn off and all that stood between the freezing air and the skin of his calf was a set of woolen BVDs, but he was free.

For the Team. For Foxx. Got to tell Foxx.

"Let him go," Chiun said. "He will not be hard to follow." He pointed to the wide indentations Riley's body had made in the snow, during his descent down the steep hill. Beyond, at the base, his footprints clearly etched the way.

REMO walked back to where the five bodies lay and opened the collar of one. "Something's funny here," he said as he read the man's dogtags. "It says that he was born in 1923. That would make him fifty-nine years old. But he's a kid. And look at this one. . . ."

"They are none of them children," Chiun said.

Remo looked at the five again. Chiun was right, he saw with amazement. *They weren't the same men he remembered killing.* The dead men possessed the same features, but all had the grizzled and aged faces of well-conditioned, middle-aged men.

"But they were young," Remo said, feeling a chill inside his bones. The smell was stronger now. It was the death-smell, but different, more stale, as if the death in these men's bodies had been sealed into a bottle for decades and finally exposed to air.

Remo bent over the soldier again. He was undeniably who the dogtags said he was: a man nearing sixty years of age. How would Remo ever explain to Smith that he had killed a nineteen-year-old boy whose body was replaced by that of a sixty-year-old man in the span of five minutes? There was something else he wanted to see. He tore the man's uniform and long underwear up to the armpit, and found it. The man's arms were covered with needle marks.

The same marks Posie Ponselle wore.

"Chiun."

They were all marked, every one of them.

"Leave them. I hear the sound of an engine." They hurtled at top speed through the snow, following Riley's footsteps. But before they reached the copse of dense pine forest where the footsteps led, the engine noise gunned to a roar and then a small Cessna appeared behind the copse. It was a low takeoff, and in the bright morning light Remo could see the pilot's face clearly. Foxx looped around in a wide circle, then buzzed directly over Remo and Chiun. As he started his ascent, he saluted Remo with two fingers and a smirk. He looped wide again and was gone.

Neither Chiun nor Remo broke the silence for several minutes. Remo held his eyes to the sky, watching the Cessna's contrails puff into fat clouds and fade away. They'd come so close. So damn close.

In a clearing in front of the airstrip Foxx had just used, Remo found the remains of an abandoned camp. Oh, sharp, Remo, he said to himself. A camp, soldiers, Foxx, the works. Right here at your fingertips. And you let them slip away. A fine assassin you are.

He went from tent to empty tent. Everything was in perfect order. Except that there were no people, anywhere. There were no vehicles, no tracks, no footprints leading out of the clearing, nothing. It was as if a small army base had just dematerialized.

"Remo." Chiun's voice came high and clear in the still air. From a distance, the old man looked as if he were dancing, prodding at the earth beside a huge pine, first with one dainty foot, then the other, his face creased in concentration. "This ground is hollow," he said.

With the heels of his hands, Remo tested the four-by-four-foot-square area Chiun had marked. Sure is," he said, clearing away the foot and a half of snow that covered it. Beneath the snow was a thick carpet of moss.

"Hah," Chiun shrieked.

"Hah? It's moss."

"It is not moss, o dim one," Chiun declared with annoyance. "This is the south side of that tree." He pointed to the towering pine. "Moss grows on the north side. This is transplanted moss. A camouflage." With one grand sweep, he yanked the patch of moss from the ground. The steel casing and combination lock of a safe lay beneath it.

Remo's face broke into a grin. "Well, I'll be. Not bad, Little Father."

"Not good," Chiun said. "Behold."

The soldiers were in the trees. There were more of them this time, armed with everything from close-range pistols to a flame thrower. The flame thrower attacked first, sending a tunnel of fire straight toward Remo.

He tore the door off the safe and held it up to the orange stream just before it reached them. Bullets pinged off the steel shield. The smell of spent ammunition filled the air. "Hold this," he said, handing the safe door to Chiun.

The safe contained a sheaf of papers—bills of sale, communications with European pharmaceutical companies, and charts. They appeared to be medical charts of some kind. At the top of each chart was a man's name, followed by a serial number. The dogtags, Remo remembered. The charts must be for the soldiers firing at him now, soldiers who had somehow found their way into Foxx's care. They detailed several years' worth of resting heart rates, stress tolerances', and a section labeled "Blood Levels" was followed by a long list of items. The first on the list was procaine. On every single chart, the procaine level of the soldier had risen dramatically during the course of the charting.

Under the last of the charts rested four manila folders. In the first was a series of photographs and a biography of General Homer G. Watson, the now-dead Secretary of the Air Force. Clipped to the biographical sheet were scores of notes detailing the general's schedules, standing appointments, and favorite restaurants. On the upper right corner of the folder was a small black *X*. The next folder contained information on Admiral Thornton Ives. The Secretary of the Navy's folder had an *X* on it, too. So did the third, belonging to Clive R. Dobbins.

"They got the Secretary of the Army," Remo said, disspirited.

"Read the news some other time," Chiun snapped. "They are boom-shooting at us, fool. Get me out of this place."

But Remo didn't move. The last dossier belonged to the president of the United States. It didn't have a black *X* on its cover. Not yet.

Remo dug back into the safe. Nothing was left in there except a series of glinting objects at the bottom. Remo reached in and pulled one of them out. It was a glass vial, about ten inches long, filled with a clear liquid and stoppered at the top by a cork. Foxx's formula, Remo thought, holding the vial up to the light. A burst of machine gun fire smashed the vial to shreds. Nothing else happened, except that someone up in the trees started wailing.

Keening, Remo thought as the high, mournful sound passed over the din of gunfire. It was more than some crazy soldier's war yell. It was a lament, high and terrible.

And then, as suddenly as it had begun, the firing stopped. "You see?" Chiun said. "You have taken so long with your library that they ran out of booms."

"I don't think so," Remo said uncertainly. "But it had something to do with this stuff." He pulled out the case at the bottom of the safe, in which the rest of the vials were stored.

"Stop!" came the high, keening voice again. "Don't break them."

Remo set the case on the ground. "What's that?"

"Don't break them. Please," the soldier shouted, scrambling down from the tree, his Centennial Airweight waving overhead. Remo recognized him as the soldier who had run away from the ambush at the lean-to. Riley threw down his gun. "Please. Leave the formula alone and we'll all come down unarmed." There was pleading in his voice.

Remo gaped in astonishment as the soldiers threw their weapons to the ground and scrambled down from the trees, each pair of eyes riveted on the case filled with glass vials.

Chiun was not surprised. "Obviously they have discovered that I was in their presence," he said smugly.

"You were behind that door," Remo objected. "They didn't even see you."

"Excuse me, o learned one. O fierce assassin. I am sure it was your excellent reading that struck fear into their hearts."

"I'll explain everything," Riley said. "Only please

. . ." He cast a baleful eye at the glass vials. "The case." He ventured toward it.

Remo snatched it away. "Uh-uh. Explain first. Then you get the goodies."

Riley hestitated. "Do you promise?" he asked. "Do you give your solemn word that you won't harm us or the case?"

Remo looked at him. The man knew where Foxx was. He could also tell a lot about the bizarre military establishment in the frozen Black Hills, where overage soldiers with the faces of kids were bivouacked. But not harming them?. . . . "Will you dump all your weapons?"

"Done," the soldier said quickly. "But it's your word, right?" He stared with something like desperation at the case in Remo's hands.

"Do you know where Foxx went?"

"Yes, I do," Riley said.

"How do I know you'll tell me the truth?"

"You've got my word on it. I'll have yours, and you'll have mine. Mine is good. What about yours?"

After a moment Remo said, "All right. We won't hurt you or the stuff. Tell your buddies to get into parade drill formation."

Riley nodded. "I'm trusting you," he said. He rounded up the apprehensive-looking young soldiers into a shambling unit in the middle of the clearing. They stood there in utter silence, every eye trained on the metal case filled with Foxx's formula.

That's what you call parade drill?" Remo said. "Even the volunteer army looks better than that."

Riley looked up, his eyes filled with anger and pride. "This is no parade unit, mister. This is the Team.

Chapter Fifteen

Randall Riley joined the Team in April 1953. He'd retired from the army with a twenty-year pension at the age of thirty-eight. At a time when most men's careers were just beginning to take off, his was over. After twenty years and two Purple Hearts, he landed a job as a dishwasher in Chicago's South Side.

Then Foxx appeared. Foxx had been in the army, too, but an earlier army, the fighters of which were now old men, far older than Foxx himself. He had flown some of the earliest American aircraft in the dogfight days of World War I.

The information came out a little at a time. During the first brief meeting at the hash joint in Chicago where Riley was working, Foxx revealed little more than a smile along with a handshake of understanding. Riley was drinking then, and fading fast. The bottle had seemed like the last refuge of a used-up combat soldier, and Foxx had understood.

"I'll be back," Foxx said. "I have a deal for you." And then he was gone.

The second time Foxx came into the restaurant was a week later. This time he arrived in a long limousine, with a hundred dollars in cash, which he handed to the besotted ex-Sergeant Riley. "This is yours whether you come with me or not. But if you come, there will be more. I plan to give you something worth more than all the money in the world."

"Whazzat," Riley asked as the two images of the man wafted in front of him in an alcoholic haze.

"Your self-respect," Foxx said.

"You from the Salvation Army or something?"

"I'm a doctor," Foxx said. "I don't belong to any organization. There's just me. If you join me, there will be two of us. But after that, there will be many, because what I am offering is a chance for you and men like you to do what they do best, for the rest of your lives." He turned to leave. "Yes or no?"

Riley put down his dishrag and followed the strange, ageless looking man. He never saw Chicago again.

That evening, they sat in the lavish dining room of the mansion near Enwood, Pennsylvania, after a meal of duckling and asparagus, hearts of palm, sole meunière, caviar, and baked Alaska. It was the grandest meal Riley had ever eaten. Afterward, he was offered a fine Havana cigar, while the butler poured a snifter of Napoleon brandy for his host.

"Think I could have a snort of that?" Riley asked pathetically.

"Absolutely not. If you agree to my contract, you'll never be permitted to drink again. It will interfere with my purpose."

Riley rose to leave. He didn't think he wanted to live in a world where every day started with a Blue Law. The butler restrained him.

"Hear me out," Foxx said, swirling the brandy temptingly in the snifter. The fire in the fireplace crackled. Through the open windows, the crisp smell of a cool April evening billowed in. "I have taken great trouble to find out about you, Sergeant Riley."

"Mr. Riley," he said bitterly. "I'm no sergeant anymore. That's over. I'm nothing but a dishwasher now. An ex-dishwasher."

Foxx raised an eyebrow. "Things are not always as they seem," he said. "As I was saying, I believe I know quite a bit about you. I know, for example, what it is you want more than anything else in life."

"Easy. A tall one with ice." He guffawed roughly.

"I'm serious, Riley. Do you know? Think. If you could have anything you wanted, *anything*, barring no consideration whatever, what would it be?"

Riley thought a moment. Then he answered with perfect honesty. "A war," he said.

Foxx smiled. "Yes. I knew you were the man I wanted."

Riley passed ten days locked in a room in that house in Pennsylvania, while imaginary bugs crawled up his legs and elephants danced on the walls. Ten horrible days that left him senseless and drained and wishing he were dead. On the eleventh day, when Riley was too weak to sit up in his vomit-covered bed, Foxx came again.

He had a hypodermic needle in his hand. "With this, you will feel better than you ever did with alcohol," he said, and injected the needle into Riley's wasted arm.

Within minutes Riley felt stronger—so strong that he thought he could snatch the sun right out of the sky.

Foxx led him outside, into the garden. "Run as far as you can," he said. "But come back. If you don't return there will be no more injections."

Riley ran. He ran for miles, past ponds and forests and a farm, which, in later years, Foxx would buy and then destroy to ensure privacy. He ran to the nearest town, some thirty miles away, and, in less than two hours after his arrival, got a job loading produce for the Enwood Market. That evening Riley started to weaken. He began to sweat profusely, and a deep feeling of panic invaded every cell of his brain. He looked in the mirror. All of the newfound vitality offered by the shot was gone, replaced with a spectral emptiness.

The next day at work his boss complained that Riley was laying down on the job, but in truth he could hardly raise his arms to lift the crates of melons and carrots. By mid-afternoon, Riley thought he was going to die.

He hitched a ride to Foxx's mansion. The driver of the car had wanted to take him to the hospital, but Riley said that his "uncle," Foxx, was a doctor. He crawled on hands and knees to the front door.

Foxx opened it, the hypodermic poised in his hand. "I thought you would come back," he said.

Riley was brought back to life, grateful and terrified. "Say, what is that stuff in that needle, anyway?" he asked, feeling his limbs come back to their former power.

"A special mixture of mine. It's based on a drug called procaine."

Riley learned that Foxx had been working on the formula for the past thirty years. With it, the ravages of time could be stopped. The young would stay young forever. Those on the brink of old age could hold off the final victory of death for all time.

"Holy cow," Riley said, filled with awe for the strange man with the magic needle. "You could make a fortune with that."

"I have," Foxx replied. "I've opened a clinic in

Europe, where rich matrons and dandies afraid of growing old come to feed their vanity. But just as you have your dream, Riley, so do I have mine.''

It was then that he told the soldier about the plan that began over the skies of Europe during the war to end all wars, before Foxx had even taken his name—he was Vaux then, a pilot.

Vaux had learned, through some recovered intelligence reports, that the U.S. Army was beginning some experiments using procaine as a base for injections that would increase the effectiveness of soldiers in combat.

He knew immediately that such a drug would change the course of history. His family, with wealth of their own, had provided for his schooling, including a diploma from medical school. But the healing of the sick held no attraction for him. What Vaux wanted to do was to fly. Flying was fun, and flying was how he passed his salad days.

But by the end of World War I, Vaux was thirty years old, and flying—what there was of it after the great aerial combats had stopped—was for the young and the foolish. Barnstorming, aerobatic displays, and the rest of the carnival-scented options open to wartime pilots during the early 1920s impressed a man of Vaux's breeding and upbringing as humiliating, akin to the plight of a great boxer forced to earn a living as a wrestler in rigged matches. Suddenly flying was no longer fun, and at thirty, the long road that stretched ahead of Vaux seemed to be filled with petty maladies and the interminable complaints of his future patients.

Like Riley, he missed the thrill of combat. His jaded appetite needed nothing less than total war to satisfy it.

And then he remembered the captured dispatches

about the procaine experiments. *Procaine.* The very word held a sort of magic. A drug that would form an army of ageless soldiers. A drug that would take an ordinary foot slog and keep him in peak physical condition for thirty years, until his long training made him the greatest soldier who ever lived. A drug that would prevent the weakening of a man's body, while his mind absorbed decades of experience. A battalion of these men, fed on procaine and trained constantly, could rule the earth.

His credentials got him into the research program almost without question. Vaux was a rich man with an impeccable background, the right training, a medical degree, and a combat record on top of it. He was a welcome addition to the staff.

But the experiments at the research center near Enwood, Pennsylvania, were progressing too slowly to suit Vaux. No one was willing to take any chances with human subjects. A guinea pig, which demonstrated remarkable capacities for stress and physical deprivation, was not enough for those scientists. Oh, no. A hundred guinea pigs were not enough. Nor a hundred cats, dogs, and Rhesus monkeys. Oh, no. Not a human, not yet. The kinks weren't ironed out, they said.

Their fears filled Vaux with unbridled disgust. The only "kink" that Vaux could see were certain unpleasant effects on the subject once the drug was withdrawn. All right, he admitted. The guinea pigs had died. But that was minor, *minor!* The procaine formula could change the face of warfare for centuries to come! He wanted to scream it.

But nothing happened. He became the most senior member of the research team, and still nothing happened. The Pentagon wanted the "kinks" to be ironed out before the drug was tried on human subjects. He was at a dead end. The army would never accept the drug unless there was a war. And then it would be too late.

"Fine," Vaux said finally in resignation after the Pentagon turned down his last request to escalate the experiments. If the army didn't want the formula, the army wasn't going to have it. The procaine—and its promise—would be his alone.

Vaux began to remove the vials of the precious mixture a little at a time from the laboratory. He was frightened of the first theft, but when no one even noticed, he took more and more. By 1937, he had removed some 1200 cases of the drug and stored it on his family's estate in upstate New York.

Then, in 1938, Germany invaded Poland, and the Pentagon now wanted procaine. It was too late, as Vaux knew it would be. A clerk with a penchant for inventory figures discovered that 1200 cases of the drug were missing. In a colossally stupid move, the government took action against Vaux, and the affair mushroomed into a fiasco that ended with Vaux's expatriation and the end of the procaine research program. The experiments were abandoned, and the research facility in Enwood sold.

It was sold, through intermediaries, to Vaux's family. And while Vaux himself was in Geneva, starting up the procaine age retardant clinic that would begin his fortune, the family quietly shipped the 1200 cases of the drug to him.

Thus began the career of Felix Foxx. With his new name and the clinic in Switzerland, he was making enough money to start an army. And if the small available supplies of procaine had to be augmented by an occasional "horse" or two like Irma Schwartz, no one would notice. His dream had begun. By the time he moved his operation back to the house in Pennsylvania, he was ready to make it a reality.

Riley trained for six weeks alone at the mansion. When he was in peak physical condition, Foxx sent him out to recruit the others for the Team.

The other members of the Team were much younger than Riley, but superior combat men, every one of them. They came from different branches of the military, and for different reasons. There was the marine who was busted for insubordination; the sailor who could outfight every man in his platoon with his bare hands; the Air Force cadet who got booted out for attacking his D.I. Later, there was the Green Beret who lost it somewhere in the jungles of Vietnam and went on a spree of indiscriminate murder from one end of the Mekong to the other. There was Davenport and a lot of guys like him. And the mercs. The mercenaries were the best of the lot. They killed because killing was what they did, and they did it without question.

Killing was the one thing that held the Team together. Every one of the men Foxx had selected knew how to kill. More important: They *wanted* to kill. In five years, Foxx had developed the beginnings of the greatest combat force in the world. The Team. And the Team belonged to him, body and soul.

Interested countries had financed Foxx and his Team right from the beginning, with shipments of gold. By 1960, the Team was ready for its first real mission. Panama hired Foxx's Team to attack the U.S. embassy on September 17. In 1963, Vietnamese President Ngo Dinh Diem was assassinated. The Team was there. In 1965, a prominent Cuban dissident met the Team on a back street in Havana. His body was found three weeks later, mutilated beyond recognition. In 1968, the dictator of a small island power carried out his own counterrevolution against his Soviet superiors. The Team stayed long enough to see a new puppet regime placed in power on the day of the funeral.

The decade passed, and then another. And whenever the leaders of a nation had required some messy business that had to be taken care of in the swiftest way possible, Foxx and the Team were called in. Every country in the world knew of the Team except the United States of America, where the Team was based.

America never knew because Foxx kept clean in America. So clean that he had written two books about diet and exercise under his new name to allay any possible suspicions and to give him a record with the IRS.

The books were a good cover. The best, and nothing but the best would do now, because a new mission had come in. The most interesting mission of them all.

Ruomid Halaffa, the strongman leader of Zadnia, had commissioned Foxx and his Team to assassinate the military leaders of the United States. This, Halaffa said, would weaken the country's military organization. Halaffa stipulated that the Secretary of the Air Force, the Secretary of the Navy, and the Secretary of the Army were to be first on the list of hits.

"What about the Secretary of Defense?" Foxx asked.

Halaffa dismissed the thought with a contemptuous wave. "A businessman," Halaffa said with a smirk. "We will leave him to his graphs and his charts. I wish to eliminate the men of might in the United States. Not a pencil pusher with his head in his behind."

Halaffa had frightened him. He was a big man, with a demented strength that seemed to emanate from his madman's eyes in waves.

"You will do this for me," Halaffa said, and it was not a request.

"Yes," Foxx answered. "I will. Is that all?"

Halaffa burst into laughter. He laughed so hard that Foxx started to laugh, too, a small hysterical titter of a laugh, until Halaffa stopped suddenly and there was nothing on his face but rage. "Fool! It is only the beginning. The real assassination will only come after you have liquidated the first three men."

"The—the *real* assassination?" Foxx asked.

"The president. You will kill the president of the United States. And then, when that odious nation has become too crippled to fight back, I will come to rule the garbage that infests that huge country and show them what a true leader is like."

Foxx shivered. Later, when he related the story to Riley, he shivered again. "His eyes," Foxx said again and again. "Crazy eyes."

"That's about it," Riley said. "He's going to Zadnia now. He'll switch to a commercial flight in Boston and reach Zadnia by tonight." The wind was gusting through the pines now, and for the first time Remo felt the chill in the air. "Can we have the drugs now?"

"Are you *nuts*?" Remo said. "After what you've told me you're going to do?"

"We can't do anything," Riley said quietly. "Foxx is gone. He didn't bring us any new supplies. Guinea pigs aren't the only things that die without the injections."

Remo looked over at the group of soldiers. They were trembling with cold. Their eye sockets looked hollow and dark. Some of the men had fainted during Riley's story. Remo thought of Posie back at Shangri-la. "Are you telling me you're going to *die*?"

Riley shrugged. "Maybe not. Maybe Foxx'll come back."

"Then I'd be crazy not to kill you now," Remo said.

One of the soldiers seemed to be strangling on his own spittle. Two others dropped to their knees, their eyes rolling. "You gave your word," Riley said.

Remo turned to Chiun. "Watch the case," he said. He went to the soldiers and methodically destroyed every weapon in sight. Then he made a body search of each man and smashed the concealed knives and guns. That still didn't eliminate the possibility of a hidden cache of weapons somewhere on the grounds.

"How long will the stuff in the case last?" Remo asked.

"Maybe five days," Riley said.

"What happens after that?"

"I don't know. Maybe there's a program somewhere, like a methadone clinic." He grinned bitterly. "More likely, we'll die. But I'd rather die five days from now, if I've got a choice." Remo studied him. "Your word," the soldier reminded him. "I kept mine."

With a wrench of indecision, Remo handed the case over. "Take off. All of you, together, up that hill." He pointed to a rounded knoll, where he could see clearly to the top. "And then keep on going. No breaks for a quickie, nothing. Just go."

"Yes, sir," Riley said. He picked up the case. Remo saw that the man's knees were wobbling. Those left standing in the crowd of sick soldiers helped those on the ground to walk, and the group shambled off together.

"You could have killed them," Chiun said.

"I know." His mouth was grim.

"You should have killed them."

Remo nodded.

"Does your word hold such importance to you?" Chiun asked, disgusted.

After a moment Remo answered, "Yes. I suppose it does."

They walked through the snow in silence. Remo knew he might have made the biggest mistake of his life. If he didn't get Foxx now, the president of the United States was going to pay for that mistake.

Chapter Sixteen

Harold Smith arrived at Shangri-la in a Grumann Air Force helicopter that touched down just outside the building. Its huge engine idled as Smith went inside.

The smell hit him as soon as he walked in the door. He gagged and blinked back the automatic tears that sprang into his eyes. Holding a handkerchief over his nose and mouth, he propped open the door, then made his way through the darkened mansion.

The place was perfectly still, silent except for the hum of the helicopter outside. The rooms were empty, their draperies drawn closed. Probably to conserve heat, he thought, eyeing the piles of ashes in each of the fireplaces. His breath came out in white plumes. But even with the cold, the stink of the place was overpowering, and growing stronger as he neared the heart of the house.

At least it wasn't summer, he thought. The last time he'd known this smell was in Korea, in a village where the North Koreans had slaughtered every man, woman, child, and article of livestock within five miles in order to "save" it from the devil Yanks. Smith was with the CIA then, and traveling with a platoon of regular army toward Pyongyang to rescue a handful of stranded agents with vital reports that couldn't be transmitted through normal channels. By the time the Americans reached the Korean village, the dead had been festering in the August sun for three days or more. The reek of death pointed the way to the village more accurately than any road sign.

In the middle of the village stood a squat mud hut. It was the only building among the strewn rubble and straw that was still standing. When Smith kicked open its woven reed and bamboo door, he was greeted by the sight of two dozen bodies, their eye sockets filled with maggots, their tongues lolling black out of their bloated faces as flies swarmed like living flesh over them.

The stink of Shangri-la brought back the image of the inside of that mud hut with a vividness that caused Smith's hands to shake. Was Remo in there? Was Chiun?

"Do your job," he muttered aloud as he hesitated a few feet in front of the arched doorway leading to the banquet hall. This was it, he knew; the smell was coming from here. He prepared himself, but as he walked inside, he knew that nothing could have prepared him for the sight in front of him.

It looked like a mausoleum. The remains of thirty people of incredible age lounged on the elegant pieces of furniture like party guests at some macabre celebration of the dead. They were dressed in finery from a dozen different eras: A flapper from the twenties, her face now a mask of withered leather beneath her bright cloche hat, sat demurely beside a World War I army major in full dress uniform, his nose a triangular hole like a jack-o-lantern's in his skeleton's face. A man in tails stared up through eyes puckered like raisins from a copy of *The New Yorker* on his lap, his bone-fingers clasped around a fresh glass of green Chartreuse. Near him, the last embers of a fire smoldered in the fireplace.

A crypt, Smith thought, taking in the rest of the room. A repository for the long dead. Except for the terrible odor of death that spewed from every crack, there was nothing to indicate that these people hadn't died decades ago. It was as if every person in the room had ceased to live long before death had actually come to claim their bodies.

In the corner, slumped over the keys of a highly polished grand piano, was a woman dressed in a shimmering white satin evening gown. An ermine stole was draped over her shoulders, and her blonde hair cascaded over the gleaming wood. Her fingers were still resting on the piano's keys.

She looks so young, Smith thought, going over to her. Maybe there was a survivor. If this one girl could remember. . . .

He lifted her by her shoulders. With a brittle snap of her neck, her head lolled back to reveal the papery, veiled face of a mummy.

With a gasp, Smith let her go. Her hand dropped again to the keyboard with a little ping of music that seemed to echo forever.

Rattled, Smith picked up his attaché case and bolted into the next room. It was empty. The kitchen was empty, too, as were the upstairs bedrooms. He was grateful. The shock in the ballroom had been enough.

He set the case on an eyelet-covered bed and used his handkerchief to wipe the perspiration off his clammy palms. When the phone inside the case rang, the handkerchief flew into the air. His stomach felt as if it had turned a complete revolution inside his body as he wiped the dried spittle from his lips and fumbled with the catches on the case.

"Yes," he said, hearing the hoarseness in his own voice.

"It's Remo. I'm at a ranch somewhere near the South Dakota Badlands." He capsulized Sergeant Riley's story, leaving out the fact that he'd released all the members of the Team. Smith would never have understood that part. "Foxx'll be in Zadnia by tonight. I've got to get over there. Now."

"Can you get me the exact coordinates of your location?" Smith asked.

"I've got them." he rattled off the coordinates.

"Hold your position," Smith said. "I'll have a plane pick you up."

"Make it a fast one," Remo said. "While you've been at home snoozing, I've been freezing my butt off in the mountains."

"I'm at Shangri-la," Smith said.

"Oh?" There was a deliberate casualness in Remo's voice. "How are the folks there?"

After a pause Smith said, "They're dead."

There was silence on the line. "All of them?" Remo said quietly. "The blonde?. . ."

"All." Smith swallowed. "We'll talk about it later. Hold your position." He hung up. His next call was to the president. Then he made an anonymous call to the local county morgue, alerting them to the presence of thirty bodies in the mansion near Enwood.

Outside, he scrambled into the helicopter and signalled the pilot to lift off. The pilot had been given instructions to follow the lemony-faced man's orders to the letter. He was a test pilot at Edwards Air Force Base who had flown every experimental aircraft brought into the base and dealt with every manner of off-the-wall order handed down by the brass, so he didn't so much as blink when he was given emergency top-security clearance to fly the Grumman to a destination known only to his civilian passenger. And he exhibited no surprise when the passenger told him to reroute the helicopter to the nearest airbase housing supersonic jets. Nor did he offer up any questions when he arrived at the base and was immediately handed a new set of top-security clearance papers to land a massive F-16 on a stretch of barren ground somewhere in western South Dakota and pick up two other civilian passengers who would direct him to his next destination. The pilot took one look at the amount of liquid oxygen and hydrogen peroxide fuel being pumped, boiling and steaming, into the F-16, and knew it was going to be a long flight, wherever he was going.

But it was all in a day's work. The pilot didn't much care who gave the orders, as long as they didn't try to fly the plane. He sat back in the flight lounge and poured himself a cup of coffee as the lemony-faced man called a taxi to take him to the nearest airport. He was probably some bureaucrat, sent to check out the efficiency of emergency operations, or some kind of nonsense like that. The two guys in South Dakota were probably doing the same thing.

The F-16 was going to be a ride and a half for them. Well, what the hell, the pilot thought. Let them have their thrill. It'll probably be the high point of their entire boring, ordinary lives.

Civilians, he thought, nodding off for a quick nap. They'll never know what real excitement is. He felt sorry for them.

Chapter Seventeen

Felix Foxx lit a slim cheroot in the anteroom to the Prince's Chamber in the Great Palace of Anatola in Zadnia. Prince Anatole had built the palace and named it, like his country's capital city, after himself. During the corrupt and pagan days of Anatole's reign before Ruomid Halaffa and a handful of treasonous soldiers deposed him in the name of justice and decency, the Prince's Chamber had been shamefully misused as a playpen, where Anatole and his confidantes carried on affairs of state through orgies of drinking and gambling and wenching with a bevy of girls imported from the deserts of the south.

Halaffa heaped scorn on the playboy prince for his wanton ways. After Anatole's execution, when the prince's bloodied head was impaled atop a minaret tower for all to see and despise, Halaffa announced the roster of sweeping changes he would bring to Zadnia. One of the main points of his stirring speech that day was that never again would the urgent matters of state be discussed in an atmosphere as besotten and sinful as the notorious Prince's Chamber.

He fulfilled his promise. During Halaffa's own orgies of drinking and gambling and wenching, absolutely no affairs of state were discussed. Discussion of affairs of state were limited to Monday morning between 10:00 and 10:30 A.M., immediately following the morning executions and just before the palace's mid-morning hashish break.

Foxx tipped the ash off the cheroot onto the floor, where it joined the mound of butts already deposited at his feet. Behind him, the gilded double doors leading to the Prince's Chamber reverberated with raucous shouting and singing and the high screams of Halaffa's concubines.

"But it's important," Foxx had told the guard at the gate, who had received instructions to send away anyone who didn't bring a bottle. "It's an affair of state."

"Come back Monday," the guard said in a nasal singsong. "Affairs of state between ten, ten-thirty."

"It's an emergency."

"Emergencies between one, one-thirty," said the guard, sounding like an Eastern bagpipe.

"This could mean world disaster," Foxx said in desperation.

"World disasters between three, three-thirty."

Foxx was frantic. "Look, I've got to see him. Aren't there any circumstances where Halaffa would see me before ten o'clock Monday morning?"

"Only super-duper emergency-casualty-world-destruction priority come before Monday morning, ten o'clock," the guard said.

"Fine. I'll take that."

"Monday morning, nine-thirty," the guard said.

At last Foxx managed, with the help of a fifty-dollar bill, to persuade the guard to escort him to the anteroom. That was six hours ago. Since then, Foxx's agitation had blossomed into the beginnings of a nervous breakdown. His hands trembled. He saw spots in front of his eyes. His mouth was dry. With every swallow the membranes of his throat stuck together like two pieces of Scotch tape.

It was *blown!* The whole beautiful, foolproof cover of Shangri-la had been discovered and somehow infiltrated by some lunatic in a tee-shirt. The man named Remo had gotten as far as the Team itself. Of course, the Team would have made short work of the thin young man and his ancient Oriental partner, but it was the principle: They knew. After almost thirty years, someone knew about the Team. And if they knew, who else might know?

It was time to go underground, to hole up in Zadnia for a year, until things blew over. He'd brought enough procaine in his plane to last him as long as it was necessary to hide out. Of course, the Team didn't have enough to get them through the next week, but he could form a new Team. It would take work, but it was possible. As for the fools at Shangri-la, there would always be more people with money, willing to trade their millions for Foxx's fountain of youth. The guests at the house in Pennsylvania were dead by now, anyway. He couldn't afford to waste time, worrying about them.

The double doors opened a crack, filling the anteroom with noise and the scent of stale smoke and whiskey fumes. Halaffa stood inside the doors, his back to Foxx, laughing and shouting in Arabic to the others in the Prince's Chamber. He was still laughing when he stepped into the anteroom.

"Your Highness," Foxx said, bowing on his knees before Halaffa. Halaffa's smile broke off and was replaced by a scowl.

"What do you want that is important enough to disturb me from the responsibilities of high office?" he bellowed.

"I seek asylum, Magnificence," Foxx squeaked. "There is a madman who has learned of our plans. He pursued me to the secret lair of my soldiers. He knows all. Perhaps he has communicated with others. The plan has been ruined. I come to you now to ask, not for payment for the three assassinations already performed perfectly, but only for a place where I may hide from the authorities of my pig-governed country until we have disappeared from the minds of those capitalist buffoons."

"I beg your pardon?" Halaffa asked.

"They're onto us. We have to—"

"Us? *We?*" Halaffa roared. "Your idiot plan goes up in smoke, and you dare to implicate *me*, Halaffa *himself?*"

"But it was your pla—"

"You are stupid enough to get caught performing treacherous acts against your country, and you expect *me* to grant you asylum?"

"Well, I only thought—"

"Where are your soldiers?"

"They're at my base, sir, your Highness, sir."

"You left them?"

"Well, this man was after me, sir, quite an extraordinary man, really. He hung out of a window—"

"You are a bigger ass than I thought. By Allah, you must be the biggest, roundest, reddest ass in the world! Are you mad? Do you think I would give even one moment's consideration to a man who would desert his own soldiers, while he flees to safety?"

"Actually, it wasn't quite that dramatic," Foxx tried to explain.

"Would I trust for one second a man who, without hesitation, would expose me and my country in a scheme that would cast us as villains the world over?"

"Oh, I think it'll all blow over in a few weeks—"

"Guard!" Halaffa screamed. "Take this vermin away. Place him before the firing squad at dawn tomorrow."

"The firing squad?" Foxx wriggled vainly to free himself from the iron grip of the two giants on either side of him. "But, Your Excellency . . . Your Worship . . . I have worked for you."

"You have failed."

"Prison, then," Foxx shouted frantically. "I'll take prison. You can't murder me just for making one mistake, can you?"

"No," Halaffa said thoughtfully. "Guards, halt." The giants stopped in their tracks. Halaffa rubbed his chin, deliberating. At last he said, "You are right, Dr. Foxx. I cannot in good conscience have you executed for abandoning your mission. After all, I am a fair man. A merciful man. A man who treads in the steps of Allah to bring peace and prosperity to Zadnia."

"Thank God," Foxx whispered. He fell to his knees. "Praise be to you for a thousand years, Your Perfectness."

"So it is my decision that you shall not be shot tomorrow morning for making a mistake."

"Your Splendidness, Your Divinity . . ."

"You will be shot for interrupting my festivities this evening. Good-bye."

"No! No!" Foxx screamed as the burly guards led him down the filthy stone stairwell into the dungeon, where rats picked clean the bones of those who had preceded him to the courtyard in which he would stand tomorrow.

After the crusted iron bars of his cell slammed shut, one of the beefy guards shook a finger at him. "Next time, wait till Monday morning," he said.

Chapter Eighteen

The pilot of the F-16 put on his best aviator's smile for his two civilian passengers as the sleek craft screamed over the Mediterranean.

"Sure sump'in' up here, idn't it?" he said in his aviator's fake Southern accent.

Chiun shrugged. "No movies," he said.

Remo focused in on the city of Anatola through the pilot's powerful binoculars. The mission. Don't think about anything but the mission now, he told himself. Posie was dead, and he might have been able to save her if . . . but don't think about that. It was over. She was dead. Period. From this distance, the city's white stucco walls and winding streets seemed almost washed clean of filth and dung and disease-bearing flies that were Zadnia's trademark the world over.

"Okay," Remo said. "You can park anywhere."

The pilot smirked behind his protective headgear. Civilians. Nonpilots. Well, who expected the lower forms of life to know beans from barnacles?

"Sorry, pal. That's Zadnia," he said.

"We know what it is," Chiun snapped. "Do you think we would fly in this noisy machine without even in-flight movies if we were going to Cleveland?"

"Fine," the pilot said, "but you can't land in Zadnia. They'll blow us up before we hit the ground."

"All right," Remo said. "That makes sense. Where do you keep the parachutes?"

"We don't have parachutes," the pilot said.

Remo shook his head. "And you'd probably lose our luggage if we had any. All right. How low can you take this thing?"

"Low?"

"Well, of course, low," Remo said. "Low."

"Right down to wave top," the pilot said.

"You don't have to go that low," Remo said. "Anything inside a hundred feet or so is good."

"What for?" the pilot asked, even as he pushed the control forward and moved the plane down toward the blue waters of the Mediterranean.

"What do you think for?" Remo asked. "Are your belts fastened?"

"Yes."

"Good-bye forever," Remo said. He punched out the plane's canopy, and then spilled out of the plane in a tumbling free fall, that quickly turned into a smooth eagle-soaring toward the white waves below.

"Sloppy," Chiun said. He moved up in his seat.

"You're not jumping, too, are you?" the pilot shouted over the scream of the wind.

"If you'd rather land. . . ."

"Can't." It was the CIA. It had to be the CIA. Some kind of nutty suicide mission, with these two ninnies the victims.

Chiun stood up.

"I wish you could take a chute," the pilot said.

"Keep your advice on my bodily functions to yourself," Chiun said, then slipped gracefully out of the jet, his yellow robe billowing in the wind like a sail.

The pilot looped once to observe the final disappearance of his two former passengers into the Mediterranean. The brass was going to want a report and a-half on this one and the details would be important.

Somehow, he noticed, the old guy in the bathrobe had managed to bring himself to the same level as the thin guy in the T-shirt.

The pilot looped again, and came in close. The two men were talking. The old one was waving his arms and shouting, while the young one shrugged and pointed up at the jet. The pilot could hardly believe it. Here they were, sailing toward the ocean, and these two loonies were having an *argument.* Then, without even taking time to scream in panic, the two crazy civilians sank into the sea at precisely the same moment.

Well, that was that, the pilot said to himself. Maybe two nuts the CIA had to get rid of. They had guts, though, he'd have to hand it to them. Neither of them had shown a trace of fear when they augured in. It had been a death worthy of an aviator.

He climbed into the sky and out of sight. Twenty seconds later, two heads bobbed out of the sea. "No movies, no lavatories, no free cakes of soap, no tea, and a foul-mouthed driver on top of it all!" Chiun shrieked. "I have had better rides in New Jersey taxicabs. How can you subject one of my delicate sensibilities to such a primitive mode of travel?"

"It was the fastest way," Remo explained for the fourth time since they'd left the F-16.

"Hurry, hurry," Chiun grumbled. "You have cast aside all the pleasures of life in the empty pursuit of speed. You have rejected the fragrance of the lotus in favor of the stench of the public bus. You have—''

"The sooner we get this over with, the sooner you can get back to your TV," Remo said.

"Can we make the eleven o'clock update?"

"Maybe."

"Stop dawdling," Chiun commanded, slicing through the water like a torpedo.

Dawn was rising in Anatola, casting pink halos around the white sun-baked buildings. Below the halos, the city's fat flies were beginning to stir, preparing themselves for another day's feasting in a land that seemed created just for them. They buzzed into the fetid streets, stopping to drink at the stagnant, sewage-laden streams that ran freely along the narrow walkways. They lit undisturbed on the delicious three-day-old cow meat, already veiled with the thick scent of decay, hanging from the hawkers' stands. For dessert, they swarmed over a tempting display of rotting fruit that would eventually be fed to the children of the wealthy after the flies had taken their fill. Another good day.

Remo swatted at the flies that buzzed in the city square like a cloud. The meat hawker scurried over to them, waving a stinking gray slab and burbling something through a mouthful of loose brown teeth.

"You've got to be kidding," Remo said, and walked on. Chiun was silent. At the gates to the city, he had slowed his breathing to a point that wouldn't even register on a life-support system. He explained that it was preferable to experiencing Zadnia and the Zadnians at full consciousness.

In the distance, the twelve towers of the Palace of Anatola stood out like needles against the reddening sky.

"Guess that's where we're going," Remo said. "You might as well bring yourself up to capacity, Little Father."

"I'd rather not," Chiun croaked.

A high wail punctuated the endless drone of the flies. At first Remo thought it was one of the vendors on the street, beginning his day's supplication to whatever idiots were desperate enough to buy the food in Zadnia, but it wasn't the call of a Middle Eastern sales-pitch. It was a cry of terror, and it was coming from inside the walled boundaries of the palace.

"He can't shoot me," the voice cried. "It's not fair. I've done everything he wanted. Be reasonable. Take the hundred. Please."

As Remo listened, a second voice, high and sing-song, came from within the wall. "When you dead, we take hundred dollah anyway. We take rings off finger. We take gold from teeth. You not have to pay us now, very welcome."

Remo scaled the palace wall and peered over. Facing the wall were twelve men in Zadnian uniforms, their weapons pointed at the solitary blindfolded figure in front of them.

"Ready," squeaked the commanding guard. The men raised their rifles.

"Inside line?" Remo whispered.

Chiun shook his head. "A waste. There are only twelve of them. We use the double-spiral air blow series."

"What for? That's a trick shot."

"Aim."

"All right," Remo sighed. "Whatever you say." He vaulted over the wall.

"Fi—aghhh." The commander's windpipe lodged into his nose as he twirled end over end above the heads of the firing squad.

"Higher," Chiun said. He grasped the rifles of two of the guards and, with a flick of his wrists, sent their owners hurtling upward before they could release their weapons. The guards, looking like khaki-colored pinwheels, flew in two different directions up to twenty feet before their trajectory curved into two huge parabolas. They met head-on in the air, their skulls cracking on impact. Chiun smiled. "A little art," he said.

"I'm glad you're enjoying yourself," Remo said, hefting the fattest soldier he'd ever seen into the air, while another attacked him from behind. "Personally, I'm getting a hernia." An inside line would have been so much easier, he thought as a soldier charged him with his AK-47. At the moment when the machinegun would have made contact, Remo was behind the guard, and then the guard was shooting forward and smashing into another, and then with a light blow to the man in front they were both airborne. Three others spiraled into the air like footballs, deflating as they impaled themselves on three of the palace's towers.

"You see now the double-spiral air blow is not so easy," Chiun said with smiling triumph.

"Who said it was," Remo grunted, propelling another guard into the palace walls.

"You did. You told all those people that I was not responsible for the beautiful attack on the two men at Shangri-la. You gave me no credit whatever."

"Chiun, look out!" Three men stood directly behind the old Oriental, their rifles leveled.

"It was masterful work," Chiun groused on without

missing a beat, as the weapons in the hands of the soldiers were suddenly buried in the dust and the men sailed upward, one after the other, in a giant oval. As each of them neared the ground, Chiun struck him upward again, bringing each blow in faster until the three men were nothing more than limp, boneless pulps, which Chiun juggled like boiled eggs.

"Okay, it's a tough attack," Remo panted, conceding the point. He flung an arm into the oval and the men crashed into a fleshy pile on the ground.

"What's going on?" came a muted, panic-filled squeak from in front of the wall.

Remo went to Foxx and pulled off the blindfold and the ropes that bound his wrists. Foxx took a look at the carnage in the courtyard, then at Remo. "You," he said, awestruck. "But I thought you were going to kill me."

"Naw," Remo said. "What's a little murder, treason, and assassination between friends? Your next target was only going to be the president of the United States. A little money in your pocket, a new government for America, run by a terrorist. What the hell?"

"I'm glad you see it that way," Foxx said, smiling.

"Just one question. Where's the procaine formula manufactured these days?"

Foxx winced. "Well, there's just a teeny problem with that," he said apologetically. "The lab in Switzerland that was producing it burned down three weeks ago. But we can get around that. Small amounts of the drug can be extracted directly from certain people. Horses, they're called, people with—"

"Yeah, I know. Like Irma Schwartz."

"Exactly." Foxx's face brightened. "They're rare, but not that rare, and it only takes six or seven bodies to produce the extract used in the mixture. It's easy, really. We can make it right at Shangri-la. I was planning to, anyway. The Schwartz woman was the first. With your skills, we can have the rest in no time."

"Great to hear," Remo said. "Just knock off a few strangers, and there you have it."

"The fountain of youth."

"Except for the poor suckers you murder just to get at the juices in their bodies."

"Nobodies," Foxx said dismissively. "Never be missed. What do you say?"

"I say there are too many amateur assassins in this world," Chiun said.

"I agree," Remo said.

"What are you two talking about?" Foxx said. "We don't need assassins. We don't need anybody, now that the three of us are a team." He gestured expansively. "The New Team, that's what we'll be. First we'll approach Halaffa and see if the deal with the president is still on. You two can take care of that one with both hands tied, I'll wager. Halaffa will love us after that."

"Wonderful," Remo said. "It'll make my whole day."

"And then I'll go to the Soviets. God knows, there are a million people the Russians want bumped off. And then there are the Red Chinese, of course."

"Of course."

"We'll make a fortune. The New Team. It's the best idea I've ever had. Think of it. Just think of it!"

"Think of this," Remo said, crushing his skull.

Foxx reeled and slumped to the ground. "So much for the New Team," Chiun said.

And then the two of them were silent, their mouths dropping open in disbelief as they watched death work a transformation on Foxx that had never been permitted in life.

As the last breath rasped out of his body, the man seemed to shrivel in front of their eyes. His skin stretched taut over the bones of his face, growing translucent and spotted with age. His eye sockets darkened and deepened to ghoulish hollows. One by one his teeth fell out, gray and cracked, and his lips whitened and puckered and sank into his flesh, like the discarded skin of a snake. In seconds, the mass of wavy dark hair on his head turned white and fell to the ground in tufts. His spine bent. His hands curled into gnarled, arthritic fists. His flesh seemed to melt away, leaving only a thin shell of withered skin over the frail bones. Foxx was suddenly old, older than anything Remo had ever seen, as old as the earth itself.

"Come," Chiun said softly. The corpse was crumbling into decay now, the bones turning to dust beneath the papery gray flesh, the eyeballs congealing into black jelly. A host of flies swarmed over it, feeding on the putrid remains.

Chapter Nineteen

Halaffa's palace was eerily still inside. There were no soldiers anywhere. No guards. The gaudy Palace of Anatola was as silent as a desert rock.

"I don't like this," Remo said as they passed through room after empty room.

"The silence of a thousand screams," Chiun mused.

The Prince's Chamber, still reeking of the festivities of the previous night, looked as if it had been abandoned in haste, its occupants vanishing in a moment of riotous merrymaking. The shouts and coarse laughter seemed still to ring in the shadows of the empty room. The stairways were empty, too. As Remo and Chiun walked up to the upper floors of the palace, the only sound was the soft flapping of Chiun's robes behind him.

There were no stirrings of life until they reached the level of the twelve towers. Chiun cocked his head at the top of the stone stairway and listened. "He is here," he said.

Remo nodded. He, too, had sensed the rhythmic expansion of air that signaled the presence of a breathing human being.

"Over here, gentlemen." The voice sounded loud as a cannon's boom after the weird stillness.

Halaffa stood in a library housed in one of the cylindrical towers. Instead of the Zadnian military uniform, which he usually wore, Halaffa was dressed in the traditional flowing robes of Zadnia's ancient nomadic tribes. On his head was a white turban with a sapphire in the center. He was a handsome man, young and swarthy, bursting with a kind of exaggerated maleness that gave an air of confidence and strength to him . . . except for the eyes.

Madman's eyes, Remo thought. They held the same look that other eyes had carried once the lust for power overcame their sanity. Idi Amin's eyes, as he starved his people to slow death. Hitler's eyes as he ordered the extermination of millions. Eyes of fire, burning with death.

"I have been preparing to welcome you," he said softly. He took a leather-covered volume from a high shelf. "Your exhibition in the courtyard was most impressive." He looked at them approvingly. "I take it you have traced the unpatriotic activities of our departed Dr. Foxx to me?"

"We have," Remo said.

Halaffa read from the book, seemingly unconcerned. "I see," he said at last. "And what, may I ask, is your purpose here?"

"We are assassins," Chiun said.

"A noble career. Then you have come here to the tower to kill me, I trust?"

"Right again," Remo said. Anytime now. His muscles screamed in readiness. Beside him, he could feel Chiun's energy coiling like a spring.

"Then step forward," Halaffa said coldly. "Make

your attempt." He slammed the book shut with a bang.

A big bang. Six bullets fired out of the thick binding directly at Remo. He dodged them, but it was a distraction. And as he was distracted, the shelf-lined walls of the tower swung open and a host of fierce-looking nomad warriors swarmed into the room, their sabers slicing through the air like lasers.

"*Now* we do the inside-line attack," Chiun said.

The sabers flew. Blood flowed like fountains over the intricate designs on the carpets in the tower room. The screams of the dying echoed down the stone stairways and empty corridors. And then all was still again.

Remo, Chiun, and Ruomid Halaffa faced one another. Halaffa's caftan was streaked with blood. His madman's eyes shone with terror and the knowledge of doom. For several moments he stood stock still, his eyes darting around the death-filled room, seeking an avenue of escape.

There was none. Only the small turret window behind him offered a way to the outside world, and that way was several stories straight down. He looked out the window. The pavement of the filthy street below was already teeming with people. They stepped laconically over the fly-studded carcass of a dead dog lying near a vendor's cart filled with melons. The city was fully awake now, already blistering under the glare of the sun.

Halaffa faced his two assailants. "You will not take me!" he shouted, then turned and scrambled onto the window ledge. "My followers will smite you with wrath. They will finish you for the vile murderers you are. They will wreak vengeance on your paltry nation."

Below, a few scattered onlookers glanced up to see their latest dictator ready to jump from a window ledge in one of the palace's twelve towers. He was shouting something. They were always shouting something. The last dictator, Anatole, shouted something before he died, too. So would the next one. The onlookers turned away and went about their business.

"Citizens of Zadnia," Halaffa bellowed. "The foes of our country have come to spread destruction and calamity in our midst. Rise up! Fight them! Fight them in the beautiful streets I have given you. Fight them in your comfortable homes, which have been my gift to you. Storm the palace and fight them as they stand ready to take your leader from you. Fight! Fight! Fight!"

"Enough of the pep talk," Remo said irritably. "Are they coming or aren't they?"

"Get up here and save my life, you miserable cretins," Halaffa yelled. "For the glory of . . . glory of . . ." His arms windmilled. "Zad . . ." he shrieked, falling off the ledge.

He landed with a thud at the base of the melon vendor's cart, next to the dead dog. The vendor, seeing the wash of blood spray onto his pulpy fruit, screeched with annoyance at Halaffa's body. The flies on the dog quickly left their old meal and swarmed onto the new delicacy that had fallen into their midst. The people on the street stepped lazily over both of them.

"Thus dies the mighty rock," Chiun said. "Crumbled to dust and lost among the forgotten sands."

Remo looked at him. "Say, that's pretty good," he said.

"An old Korean saying." He stepped across the bodies strewn around the room and lifted a large painting of Halaffa framed in ornately carved gold.

"This will do nicely," he said.

"You want a picture of him?"

"Of course not," Chiun said. With his thumbnail he etched four lines along the sides of the protrait, then punched it out. He handed the empty frame to Remo. "For you," he said.

Remo stared at the strange gift. "Well, thanks, Little Father, but I really—"

"It will make a nice frame for my picture of Cheeta Ching."

Remo groaned.

"In Korean dress," Chiun said.

Chapter Twenty

Harold W. Smith sat at his desk in front of the computers at Folcroft Sanitarium, looking even more lemony than usual. In front of him was a tangle of green and white striped printouts.

"Where is Remo?" he asked, his voice acid.

"He will be here shortly," Chiun said.

Smith shook the sheaf of paper on his desk. "Fifteen old soldiers dressed in World War II military uniforms were found dead of various symptoms of old age in the Black Hills of South Dakota this morning," he said. "Do you know about this?"

"Should I?" Chiun asked innocently.

"They died of old age," Smith repeated.

Chiun shrugged. "We all have our time."

"This was the Team, wasn't it?" he sputtered. "Foxx's Team. Remo didn't kill them. They were under orders to murder the president of the United States, and he didn't kill them. That's the truth, isn't it?"

Chiun sighed. "What do I know," he said philosophically. "I am but an old man, a being in the twilight of his years, who wishes only for a small ray of beauty to bring light into the weary darkness of his life. My one

195

request to you, O mighty Emperor, was of a small photograph of the lovely Cheeta Ching in the timeless garb of her native land. But lo, even that humble request was denied. And I accept that denial. I am but an unworthy assassin whose knowledge is unwanted. I am but a small grain upon the pebbled beach of life. . . ."

"Oh, never mind," Smith said.

"Goddammit, I'm going to fry your ass," snarled Cheeta Ching as Remo tied the rope around her wrists into a neat square knot. Her feet were bound to the legs of the Bauhaus chair in Cheeta's living room furnished in early Gestapo. Remo still felt the bruises from that maneuver. The way the woman kicked, Remo reasoned she'd received her journalistic training in the Viet Cong.

In the scuffle, he managed to drag her into the flowing red and yellow satin robes he'd rented from a costume shop, but she'd slugged her way out of them three times, and by the time the newscaster was adequately restrained, the gown was a mass of tatters held together with several rolls of shiny scotch tape.

"I told you, I just want to get a picture," Remo said.

"Then call my press agent, asshole. From jail. Breaking and entering's a crime in this state, you turkey."

"Yes, well, I'm sorry about that," Remo said, adjusting his camera, "But I did ask you. And your agent. You both refused."

"Damn right, shitheel," Cheeta screeched. "Some pervert wants me to pose for him in this wierd getup straight out of a road show of Gilbert and Sullivan, what do you expect?"

"A picture," Remo said patiently.

"I suppose you're going to rape me next."

"Wrongo," Remo said. "Smile."

"I know what you scumbags have on your minds. You see a gorgeous chick, all you want to do is whack it to her."

"I'll decide that if I happen to see one," Remo said. "You're drooling."

Cheeta seethed. "You know what you are?"

Remo sighed, advancing the film. He was going to get a whole roll of the harpy in all her glory, so that Chiun would have his choice of twenty-four different aspects of the nastiest human being on earth. And Remo would never have to return. "No. Tell me."

"You're a sexist, capitalist, imperialist, warmongering swine," she said, grinning triumphantly.

"Great," Remo said, snapping off two shots. The old man would like the smiling pictures. "What else?"

"Huh?"

"Tell me what else I am."

She thought for a moment. "A foul, disgusting, loathsome degenerate?" she asked tentatively.

"Fine, fine," Remo said, snapping away. Those expressions would pass for Serene Contemplation. "How about an obnoxious, offensive, vile, inhuman beast?" he offered.

Cheeta brightened. Her face came as close to innocent joy as it was ever going to get. "Hey, that's okay, really okay. You ought to go into the news business. There's lots of opportunity for creative writing in the news."

"So I've noticed," Remo said. "Go back to calling me an imperialist warmonger. You look better that way."

"How dare you talk to me like that, you seedy, revolting, shit-brained clod."

"Terrific," Remo snapped off a few more. " 'Seedy's' good. Works almost like 'cheese.' "

"You don't know your pecker from a stick," Cheeta sneered.

Remo snapped. "Sure I do," he said pleasantly. "I'd touch you with a stick."

Cheeta emitted a high jungle yell. " ''You sick, slimy, nauseating, vermin-infested, flee-bitten, loose-boweled, crap-eating jock-honkey-nigger-kike jerk-off!" she screamed.

Remo finished off the roll. "That did it. You're a natural, Cheeta. You ought to pose as a centerfold. *Soldier of Fortune* might be interested. They like pictures of tanks. Be seeing you."

She strained on the ropes behind her back, jumping so hard that the chair thumped off the gouund. "Hey, you can't leave. Get me out of this thing. Untie me."

"I'll call your keeper," Remo said.

Chiun hung the picture in a place of honor directly in front of the window in the motel room. It blocked out most of the light.

"This way, when we seek the sun, we will find it behind Cheeta's bright visage," he said.

"Great," Remo said, squinting up from the book he was straining to read. "She looks better in the dark, anyway."

He went back to his book. It was a history of the film goddesses of the thirties. The pages on Posie Ponselle were worn and shiny. For the thousandth time, Remo stared at the old photograph of her, looking exactly as she did the last time he saw her.

"You have pleased me, my son."

"I'm glad, Little Father," he said quietly. Nothing was going to bring Posie back now. Maybe that was for the best. She herself had told him that there were worse things than growing old, and she probably knew what they were. But he missed her. He couldn't help that.

"You have gladdened my heart almost to perfection."

"It's okay, Chiun."

"I say almost, because there is but one other thing, a small thing, a nothing, that would make my happiness complete."

Remo didn't answer.

"I said there is but one other thing," Chiun said, louder.

Remo looked up, disgusted.

"Of course, if you have no thought of an old man's final happiness in the twilight of his years . . ." He trailed off. Remo went back to his reading. "It would have been such a small request," Chiun went on. "A mere trifle. The humblest of insignificances—"

"Oh, hell," Remo said, slamming the book. "What is it?"

The old man's face beamed with fresh anticipation. "I was just thinking, Remo," he said, bouncing as he spoke, "how lovely it would be to have a picture of both of us. Of the lovely Cheeta Ching and the Master of Sinanju together. Perhaps with her small delicate hand clasping mine as she gazes up to me in adoration. Something simple. With the romantic shores of Sinanju in the background. Remo . . . Remo? Where are you going?"

"Ever hear of the Foreign Legion?" Remo asked at the door.

"No."

"Good."